THE ASSASSIN AND THE BEAR

THE SHIFTERS SERIES
BOOK NINE

ELIZABETH KELLY

EK PUBLISHING INC.

Edited by:
L. Nunn Editing

Cover art by:
EK Designs

THE ASSASSIN AND THE BEAR

Tori knows she shouldn't flirt with the sexy bear shifter, Judd. She's a bunny shifter. There's no future for them. And not just because he's a predator and she's prey.

Tori isn't nearly as prey-like as Judd thinks she is…

She's hidden behind her dumb bunny façade for so long that she's almost forgotten who she really is.

Until an old enemy finds her.

With hiding no longer an option, Tori prepares to make her final stand. But with danger lurking around every corner, she'll need Judd's help as well as a little magic.

Judd's wanted Tori from the first day she started working at the bar. Too bad the flirty bunny shifter has made it clear they'll never be anything more than friends.

Until he sees the real Tori, and everything changes.

Judd is thrust into a treacherous world of magic, mad scientists, and a sweet little bunny shifter who just might be an assassin.

With the fate of the world at stake, will Judd convince Tori that they can save the world and build a life together?

CHAPTER 1

Astoria Genevieve Baker did not have time for the bullshit currently going down just a block from her shitty apartment.

She'd be lucky if she weren't late for her work shift as it was.

Of course, it didn't mean she would walk right by the woman's soft cries like the asshole ahead of her had done. Fuck that bullshit.

Her boss was a good guy. He'd forgive her for being late this one time.

She turned down the mouth of the alley, marching steadily toward the bastard who had the woman pinned against the wall and was currently slapping her face in a steady rhythm that was more about the humiliation than the pain.

Astoria sniffed the air. The dickweed was a skunk shifter. The odour that clung to every pore would have clued in even a human. The woman was a skunk shifter too. Unsurprisingly, skunks tended to stick to their own kind, mostly because of the smell.

She slipped from her jacket, letting it fall to the snow-covered ground. The cold air bit into her bare arms and seeped past her nylon-clad legs, but she ignored it. A little cold wouldn't hurt her.

As Astoria grew nearer, she could hear his whiskey-roughened voice say, "You gonna disrespect me again, Carla?"

"No, Bill, I won't. I promise." The woman's voice cracked every time Bill's palm connected with her cheek.

"Good, because I'm getting fucking sick and tired of -"

"Hey, dick for brains!" Astoria's voice was soft but clear.

Bill didn't turn away from Carla, although he did stop slapping her. "Get lost, bitch. This ain't any of your concern."

"Did you come out of your mama this fucking ugly, or did you get smacked in the face with a baseball bat?"

Lame. She really needed to work on her insult game.

It may have been lame, but it caught Bill's attention. He stepped away from Carla. The skunk shifter stayed where she was… huddled against the wall, her cheeks bright red from the slaps and tears forming ice chips in the dark hollows under her eyes.

"What the fuck did you just say to me?" Bill said.

He started toward her. He was a big man, probably just past the six-foot mark, with a soft belly and jowls beginning to sag. He towered over her diminutive size. Not that she gave a fuck. The bigger they were, the harder they fell, right?

She rolled her shoulders like a boxer before a big fight and cracked her neck as Bill grew closer. It'd been a long time since she'd been in a fight, and she wondered if she still had it in her. Fighting was a lot like dancing. The less you practiced, the rustier you got.

It was too late to worry about it now. Bill was nearly on

her, and from the look on his face, he was getting ready to start slapping her around like poor Carla.

Bill stopped inches from her, staring down at her with a sneer. He sniffed in her direction before looking her up and down, his gaze lingering on the tight, thigh-high skirt she wore and the t-shirt that clung to her perky tits like a second skin. "You're not half bad looking, are you, ya little slut? Tell you what, I'll forgive you for the disrespect you just showed me 'cause I can be a nice guy. So, hop away, little bunny, this ain't none of your fucking concern."

He turned around to head back to Carla. Astoria shot her leg out, kicking him in the ass with the toe of her winter boot. It made a satisfying, meaty thud, although Bill's pig-like squeal as he staggered forward was infinitely more enjoyable.

He turned around. The shock on his face made her laugh, and Bill's surprise quickly turned to rage. His face red and chest heaving, he came at her with his fists raised and murder in his eyes.

She dodged his first wild swing with practiced ease, her body doing what came naturally despite how long it'd been since she'd fought. His following two punches were just as simple to avoid. His anger and shock worked against him, although she would have kicked his ass easily, even if he'd been clear-headed.

She taunted him for a few minutes, letting him try to hit her at least half a dozen times as she dodged and ducked. He repeatedly swore, his fists flying, but she was a rabbit, for fuck's sake. She was built for speed.

"You little bitch, stop fucking moving!" he growled out.

She laughed again. "What's the matter, stinky pants? You too old to catch me?"

"You slut!" he shouted.

She ducked out of the way of another wild swing. "You know slut isn't an insult, right?"

"I'm gonna rip your fucking legs right off your body," he said.

"You'd have to catch me first, slowpoke," she said with another taunting grin.

He roared with anger. She side-stepped him neatly when he rushed forward, sticking her foot out and grinning when he tripped over it and sprawled into the snow. He jumped to his feet, snow and… ew, gross… a rotting banana peel stuck to one cheek.

"Uh," she pointed at his face, "you got a little something…."

He swiped the peel off his face with another angry roar. Astoria could have done this all day, fuck, it was incredible how good this felt, but she really would be late if she didn't finish this in the next few minutes.

Bill rushed toward her again – some assholes just never learned – but this time, she grabbed the lid of a trash can with her right hand and blocked Bill's blow with her left arm. Before he could swing at her again, she punched him in the face with the garbage lid. The crunch the metal made when it connected with his nose sent a wave of satisfaction over her.

Bill the skunk crumpled to the ground, his legs folding under him like a wobbly card table, and his eyes rolling up in his head as blood gushed from his broken – well, more like shattered – nose.

She leaned down and studied his face before giving him a boot to the ribs. He didn't move, and she dropped the trash can lid beside his prone body and turned to Carla.

"You okay?"

Carla blinked at her before pushing away from the wall and joining her on unsteady legs. "You… you killed Bill."

"Nah, he's not dead. Just unconscious. Although…" Astoria leaned down and heaved Bill's body onto his side so he wouldn't choke to death on his own blood. She might not be opposed to beating the fuck out of some slimy shithead who liked to slap women around, but she wasn't a killer.

Not anymore, anyway.

Carla still stared at Bill, like she couldn't believe what had happened. "I… thank you."

"You're welcome," Astoria said. "Hey, this isn't my business, but you can do better than this loser. You know that, right?"

"It's my fault," Carla said. "I wore something I shouldn't have, and I knew Bill wouldn't like it." She pointed to the skinny jeans she wore. "My pants are too tight, and I showed too much cleavage at -"

"Don't do that," Astoria said. "You're allowed to wear whatever the fuck you want to wear. It's your body. Don't let this asshole," she kicked Bill again, grinning when he groaned in pain despite still being unconscious, "convince you he has the right to tell you what to do with your body or your life for that matter. He has no power over you."

Shit, now she sounded like an after-school special, but damn if she didn't hate to see a woman looking broken and defeated over a fucking man.

Carla stared at her. "My sister says the same thing."

"You should listen to your sister."

Carla pulled out her phone and snapped a picture of Bill's face. She smiled at Astoria. "For my sister. She'll probably frame it and hang it on the wall."

Astoria laughed and walked to the front of the alley to snag her coat. Carla followed her and patted her arm a bit timidly. "Seriously, thank you for helping. Where did a bunny learn to fight like that?"

"You're welcome." She ignored the second question. "Do you live with Bill?"

Carla nodded. "I do. Or rather, I did. I'm about to grab my shit and take the next bus to my sister's. She lives in Winchester. You ever been there?"

"Once. In another life," Astoria said. "Take care of yourself, Carla."

"You too."

Carla headed north, and Astoria kept going south to her car parked on a side street. She climbed behind the wheel and turned the heat high, rubbing her hands together to warm them up. Her rabbit bounced around with glee, and Astoria couldn't help but grin at her excitement.

We should find someone to fuck. C'mon, pretty please? Her rabbit pleaded.

She shouldn't have been surprised that the rush of adrenaline from the fight had turned into a serious need to fuck. She was a rabbit shifter, after all. Still, her libido could and often did get her in trouble, and there'd been more than one occasion when she'd wished she had better control of it.

It was only a fifteen-minute drive to work, but she was still five minutes late when she parked in the half-full lot and hurried toward the entrance. She stopped and took a few deep breaths, trying to calm the adrenaline rush and her urge to fuck.

It had lessened slightly in the drive to work, but it would roar back to life the minute she saw him.

It always did.

She and her rabbit both wanted him with a raw intensity that grew harder and harder to ignore. Working with him day in and day out certainly didn't help, nor did his flirty behaviour or the lust she could sometimes smell drifting from his skin when he looked at her.

That got her rabbit worked up something awful, but she'd never read too much into it. He was a natural flirt. She'd seen his flirting skills in action many times, and it was never a surprise to her when the women lapped it up. She understood it. Hell, most shifts, she could barely stop herself from pushing him into the supply room and riding him like a pony.

Shit, she needed to stop thinking about him and his body, or she really would lose control. Maybe she'd get lucky. Maybe he wouldn't be right at the front door, and she wouldn't have to hear his deep voice, smell his intoxicating scent, or be knocked over by his two-hundred-watt grin. His shift started at the same time as hers, but he could be in the back room grabbing a keg. He was technically the bouncer but helped with other stuff at the bar.

She rolled her shoulders again, arranged her face into her usual mask of brainless innocence, and mentally submerged herself in the role of the dumb bunny she had perfected. She opened the door and stepped inside the warm bar, making sure her smile didn't slip when *he* was right there.

"Hello, doll." His warm and appreciative look stripped her to her very core despite her layers of clothes.

What was it about this man that made her want to throw away her new life and show him who she truly was? No matter what it cost her.

"Oh, like, hey, Judd. How ya doin', handsome?" The affected Valley Girl voice she had adopted grated on her nerves, just like it always did.

"Can't complain, sweet thing. You're looking gorgeous tonight," Judd said.

"Oh my God, stop it! You're making me blush." She giggled, making it so high-pitched that the wolf shifter in the corner booth glanced over with a look of irritation.

"How was your day? You do anything fun with the kids?"

7

Judd shoved his hands into his back pockets, making his t-shirt cling to his chest and sending her lust into overdrive. Her rabbit was going crazy, and sweat dripped down her back as she fought for control.

Judd could smell her lust. He was a black bear, and they had great sniffers. But what did it matter? He knew she lusted after him, but he also knew she wouldn't fuck him. He'd apparently made peace with that long ago and was content to keep things flirtatious.

Which didn't bother her. Nope, it didn't bother her one little bit.

Maybe if she kept telling herself that, she'd eventually believe it.

"It was, like, fine. The kids had a birthday party to go to this morning." The lie about her non-existent children rolled easily off her tongue.

"I didn't do much while they were gone because I was sooo tired from last night's shift, and, like, my feet were totally killing me. I really need to get some better arch support in my shoes. You know? Like, I heard that most women are nearly crippled by the time they're forty because the shoe manufacturers deliberately use this weird material in the insides of their shoes that make women's feet change shape over time. Isn't that, like, terrible?"

"I haven't heard that," Judd said.

She could barely stop the laughter – her genuine laugh, not that fake giggling shit she did and fucking hated – from spilling out. One of the things she loved about Judd was his ability to keep a straight face when she droned on and on. Not only that, but he actually appeared to pay attention too.

"Yeah, I know it's, like, kind of crazy, but -"

"Tori!"

She looked to the bar where her boss, Porter, stood near the beer kegs. "You're late."

"I gotta go, big guy." Knowing she shouldn't, but fuck, she was *dying* over here, she let her hand trail across Judd's flat, tight abdomen. Just the feel of his hard stomach made her fucking gush into her panties. "I'll talk to you later, okay?"

"You bet, Tori-girl." Judd winked at her.

Telling her rabbit to simmer the fuck down, she walked away.

CHAPTER 2

The chipmunk shifter was gonna be a fucking problem.

Judd knew it, Porter knew it, hell, even Alfie knew it, and he'd been a bouncer at the bar for less than two weeks.

Judd settled back against the bar, watching the chipmunk as he pushed past a group of badgers who, based on their business suits and the lanyards around their necks, were a part of the big environmental conference happening at the hotel down the street.

The chipmunk bumped the smallest badger as he shoved past him, spilling the badger's beer onto the front of his fancy suit. The badger snarled and whipped around. "What the fuck?"

Judd tensed, pushing away from the bar as the chipmunk glared at the man. "You got a fucking problem with me, buddy?"

The badger glanced at his friends, saw no help, and backed down immediately. "No, I don't."

Judd didn't blame him. Badgers were tough as fucking nails, but going after the chipmunk was pure insanity. The chipmunk shifter was only about 5'8", but, like ninety-five percent of chipmunks, he hit the steroids hard along with Christ only knew what other muscle-enhancing poisons he'd pumped into his body. The drugs bulked up the chipmunks, but they made them mean, unpredictable, and as nasty as those fucking Canadian geese.

"That chipmunk's gonna be a problem." Alfie leaned against the bar next to Judd.

"Tell me something I don't fucking know." Judd glanced at the leopard shifter. "You ever had to deal with a chipmunk before?"

"At the security place I worked for a few years back, we used to patrol a local mall. Had trouble with a chipmunk in the food court. The Dixie Chicken got his order wrong, and he lost his fucking shit. They called me and my partner, Vince, to escort him out of the mall. He didn't want to leave, and shit went downhill real fast."

"What happened?"

Alfie scanned the bar, his lean body on high alert as he tracked the chipmunk's progress across the crowded space. "Vince is a brown bear and fucking tough. We got him into cuffs, but the asshole shifted to his chipmunk, ran up Vince's pant leg, and chomped on his fucking balls."

Judd's mouth dropped. "You're kidding me?"

"Nope. Vince says he still has tooth marks on his sack."

"Fucking chipmunks," Judd said.

"Fucking chipmunks," Alfie agreed.

They both turned at the growling from the booths along the bar's right side. A snake shifter and a mongoose shifter were shoving at each other's chests, and Judd rolled his eyes. "For fuck's sake, those two were just in here last night and got into a fight then too."

"I've got it," Alfie said. He pushed through the crowd as Judd looked for the chipmunk again. A growl erupted from his chest, and he immediately stalked across the bar. His bear snarled and growled, and Judd didn't try to calm him down.

It was useless to try. The chipmunk was touching Tori, and even if his bear couldn't see how the chipmunk shifter's fingers were sinking into the soft meat of Tori's upper arm, he would have been pissed. Lately, his bear got pissed when anyone even looked at Tori. And considering that Tori was the most beautiful woman in the bar on a nightly basis, a lot of fucking men looked at her. His bear spent most of their work shifts in a terrible mood.

His bear snarling and snapping, Judd stopped beside them and stared at the chipmunk. "Take your fucking hands off of her."

"Get lost," the chipmunk said without looking at him. He squeezed Tori's arm until she gasped. "I said bring me another beer, you stupid little bitch."

Judd had to give it to Tori. Even for a rabbit shifter, she was on the tiny side, but she stared the chipmunk in the face and said, "And I said you're cut off, you dense cabbage."

Judd's grin died when the chipmunk shook Tori so hard that the tray of beers she carried crashed to the floor, spraying his boots with liquid. His bear roared deafeningly, and the chipmunk made a strangled yelp when Judd's hand shot out and wrapped around his thick neck.

Judd squeezed hard, baring his fangs at the chipmunk as a deep growl radiated from his chest. "Take your fucking hand off of her."

The chipmunk choked and gagged but didn't release his grip on Tori. Judd leaned in closer, his bear snarling and growling at him to kill the man, and said, "Take your fucking hand off of her now, or I will string you up by your nutsack, rip out your fucking intestines, and use them as skipping rope. Do you understand me?"

The chipmunk released Tori. His face was bright red, and he clawed at Judd's hand as Judd's bear pushed forward and goaded Judd into saying, "I think I'll fucking kill you anyway, you rancid dickmeat."

"Judd, enough."

Judd barely heard Hudson's voice over the angry demands of his bear.

Kill him for touching her. Kill him!

His bear had the right idea. The prick chipmunk was about to discover what happened to assholes who thought hurting innocent women was acceptable. Who thought hurting *Tori* was acceptable.

"Judd, let him go." Hudson's big hand clamped down on his shoulder.

Judd snarled at his best friend, baring his fangs as his bear pushed for control. "He fucking touched her."

"I know, but if you kill him, you'll go to prison, you idiot. So fucking let him go." Hudson was doing a great job as the voice of reason, but Judd and his bear were about two hundred yards past reason. All that mattered was making sure the chipmunk and everyone else in the bar knew that hurting Tori resulted in a very fucking painful death.

"Judd." Tori's arm wrapped around his waist, and her tiny hand patted his lean stomach. "It's okay, big guy. Let him go."

"He hurt you," he snarled.

"I'm okay. I promise." Her voice was soft and low. It didn't sound at all like her usual high-pitched Valley Girl voice, and a shudder of pure need went through him. Christ, he wanted her so fucking bad.

"Let him go, Judd," she said, rubbing her hand back and forth across his stomach.

He released the chipmunk shifter, and the guy immediately bent over, hacking and coughing before falling to his knees. He wheezed in a breath. "I'm gonna fucking sue you. I'm gonna...."

Hudson reached down and hauled him to his feet. The chipmunk shifter might have been used to intimidating other shifters with his muscles and his attitude, but Hudson was a polar bear shifter. He was over seven feet tall and thick with muscle, and even a steroid-abusing, rage-filled chipmunk shifter would be insane to go after him.

The chipmunk stared up at Hudson as the polar bear shifter leaned down and said, "What you're gonna do is get the fuck outta this bar and never come back."

"You can't kick me out," the chipmunk shifter's voice was hoarse, and he rubbed at his throat, "you're just the fucking bartender."

"Yeah, well, I'm the fucking owner, and I can kick you out." Porter, the wolf shifter who owned Bud's bar, stood beside Hudson. "Do what the bartender said and get the fuck out of here. You're banned, asshole."

"Fuck all of you!" The chipmunk shouted before stalking toward the door. He shoved it open and disappeared into the darkness.

"You all right, Tori?" Porter studied the red marks on her arm.

"I'm good, Porter." Tori's voice sounded normal again, and she smiled up at Judd before squeezing him. "Thanks so much, big guy. You're, like, my hero tonight."

His bear chuffed to her, and Judd swallowed the sound. "You should get your arm checked out at the hospital."

She giggled and slapped him playfully on the stomach. "It's, like, not that bad, silly." She stood on her tiptoes and brushed her lips across his cheek. "Thank you, handsome."

"You're welcome, Tori-girl," he said as she glanced at the mess of broken glass and spilled beer.

"I, like, need to get a mop before someone slips in this," she said. She walked away, and Judd studied her perfect ass in her tight skirt as Porter returned to his office.

"Jesus, your lust is so thick right now that a human could smell it." Hudson clapped Judd on the back. "I seriously don't get what you see in the bunny."

"Tori's sweet," Judd said.

"She doesn't have a single brain cell in her head," Hudson said.

"So fucking what?" Judd said. "Doesn't mean she deserves to be treated like she's second class."

"I didn't say she did," Hudson said. "What's gotten into you tonight?"

"Nothing," Judd said. "I'm just…tired."

"I don't get why you don't just fuck her and get her out of your system," Hudson said.

"She doesn't want to fuck me," Judd said.

His bear made an undignified whine that Judd ignored.

"Of course she wants to fuck you. She's a rabbit shifter," Hudson said.

Judd glared at him, and Hudson held up his hands. "I'm not insulting her. It's a well-known fact that rabbit shifters aren't picky when it comes to fucking."

"Yeah, well, she's made it clear she's not into me," Judd said.

Hudson squatted and began to pick up the bigger pieces of broken glass with his ham-sized hands. "Smells like she's into you."

Judd bent and picked up glass pieces as well. "Fine. She's into me, but she doesn't want to fuck me."

Hudson sniffed the air, and a rare grin crossed his face.

16

They both straightened, and Judd didn't need to turn around to know that Hudson's mate was behind him. The happiness on Hudson's face said it clearly.

Hudson's polar bear growled and chuffed before Hudson said, "Hello, my mate."

"Hi, honey."

Judd turned and smiled at the tall and curvy human standing behind him. She held a large plastic container in her hands, and the delicious scent of lasagna drifted from it. "Hi, Rosalie. How are you?"

"I'm good, Judd. You?"

"Can't complain," he said.

She studied the broken glass in his and Hudson's hands before smiling at Hudson. "I brought you dinner, but I can leave it and head home if this is a bad time."

Hudson shook his head. "No, I can take my dinner break now."

He handed the broken pieces of glass to Judd, barely glancing at him as he put his hand against Rosalie's lower back and ushered her toward the large employee's only booth near the back.

Judd squatted to pick up more glass, smiling at Carmen when she stooped beside him and grabbed the last broken glass. "Thanks, Carmen."

"Of course." She gave him a toothy grin as they both straightened. Like Alfie, Carmen started at the bar a few weeks ago. She was a capybara shifter, and her body was thick with muscle. Her reddish brown hair was short and spiky, and she was calm and easygoing.

She swept her gaze over his body, and he could smell the faint scent of her lust for him. "You didn't get hurt, did you?"

"By a chipmunk shifter? Fuck, no," he said.

She laughed as she followed him to the garbage bin

behind the bar, and they dumped the broken pieces of glass into it. "How was your day off yesterday?"

"Good," he said. "Didn't do much. How about you?"

"I met up with a few friends and went swimming at Clove Lake. We're going again on Thursday. You should join us."

"Isn't it supposed to be below zero on Thursday?" Judd asked.

"And snow." Alfie leaned against the bar again. He had a slight cut on his face, and his dark brown hair was messed up. "Not to mention the Solum Winds. They're a hell of a lot stronger outside of the city. They'll cut like a knife right through you."

Carmen shrugged before smiling at Judd. "You can always swim in your animal form if it's too much for your human side."

"Thanks, but I think I'll pass."

"Suit yourself," she said with another grin. "But if you change your mind, you know where to find me."

She walked away with a sexy sway to her ample hips that Alfie watched with appreciation. "I hate to see her leave, but I love to watch her go."

Judd snorted. "Lame, Alfie."

Alfie laughed. "Yeah, I know. Are you going to sleep with her?"

"Carmen?" Judd said.

Alfie dabbed a bar napkin against the cut on his cheek. "Don't say it like that. You know she wants you."

Judd shook his head. "I'm not going to sleep with her."

"Cool. So, you won't care if I do, then?" Alfie asked.

"Why would I?"

"Just wanted to make sure it wasn't a Tori situation."

"What the fuck does that mean?" Judd asked.

Alfie balled up the napkin and tossed it in the garbage

bin. "It means that if I slept with Tori, you'd have my balls on a keychain."

"Tori and I aren't... I mean... she's free to sleep with whomever she wants," Judd said.

"And yet, she doesn't."

Judd glanced at Tori, who was mopping up the spilled beer. Alfie clapped him on the back. "I may have only been here a couple of weeks, but it's obvious you're totally into each other. Fuck, I knew it within the first half hour of my first shift. Weird, though. I've never seen a rabbit shifter lust after someone like she lusts after you without actually fucking them."

Stupidly, hurt rolled over Judd, and Alfie sniffed the air before squeezing his shoulder. "Shit, man, that came out wrong. I didn't mean it like that. It's just, you know, rabbit shifters and their libido... they're not known for their restraint."

"Yeah, I know. C'mon, we need to get back to work. Porter isn't paying us to talk," Judd said.

CHAPTER 3

T ori peeled off the rubber gloves and tossed them in the cleaning bucket before throwing both into the supplies closet. Despite her gloves, she scrubbed her hands with hot water and the industrial-sized bottle of soap sitting next to the deep sink in the closet.

The sour smell of vomit lingered in her nostrils, and she leaned against the wall next to the shelf of cleaning supplies. Fuck this night. It'd been a fucking disaster since she stepped into the bar. She grimaced and rubbed at her forehead. The temptation to walk straight to Porter's office and tell him she quit was overwhelmingly strong. Being a server wasn't exactly her fucking dream job, and cleaning up a shockingly large amount of puke in the ladies' bathroom was one hell of a way to end her shift.

She straightened and paused with her hand on the door handle. Quitting her job, as tempting as it was, wasn't the answer. She might hate being a waitress, but she liked eating and having a roof over her head.

So find something else. Anything else! Work for Porter's

brother - the one who owns the security firm. It's much more suited to your skills.

Yeah, it was, but it was also the first fucking place *he'd* look for her. And he was still looking for her. She couldn't fool herself into thinking she was safe. That almost got her killed the last time he found her.

She yanked open the door and walked down the hallway. Ten more minutes and Porter would close the bar, and she could cash out and go the fuck home. She'd have a hot bath and a -

"Well, hey, pretty bunny. I've been looking for you."

She groaned but plastered on a smile as the tiger shifter walked out of the men's room. He did a zipper check before adjusting his crotch, his grin widening when her gaze dropped to the motion.

She rolled her eyes internally. The tiger shifter had been hitting on her all night, and she was fucking over it. Still, she kept that false smile firmly in place as the tiger leaned on the wall before her. "You disappeared on me."

"Oh, like, I was cleaning up so much vomit in the ladies' room." Her Valley girl voice annoyed the tiger, she could smell it on him, so she amped it up to a thousand. "It was, like, soooo gross. But, like, you know, it's totally part of my job."

"Right." The tiger shifter trailed his finger down her bare arm. "So, the bar's closing soon. What do you say I wait for you in the parking lot, and we go somewhere a little more private."

"Oh, like, aren't you just the sweetest!" She giggled and patted his arm. "But my kits are, like, waiting at home for me, so…."

"They can wait a little longer." His finger investigated the sliver of flesh between her tank top and skirt. "You've been coming on to me all night, sweet thing. Don't play shy now."

Her patience died along with her false smile, and she dropped the Valley girl accent. "No, I fucking wasn't."

The tiger shifter blinked, his pupils narrowing as a low hiss escaped his throat. "What did you say?"

"I said no, I fucking wasn't. You're just so fucking arrogant you think any woman being nice to you means she wants to bone you."

"You bitch," the tiger shifter said. "I gave you fucking amazing tips all night."

" Let me give you a tip - when a waitress flirts with you, it's because she wants your money, not your dick." Tori pushed past the shifter.

With a low growl, he grabbed her arm and yanked her back to him. "No one fucking talks to me that way. Especially not a dumb little bunny who doesn't have a single thought beyond who's she gonna fuck next. Now, are you gonna play nice and apologize, or do I have to - FUCK!"

The tiger shifter bellowed in pain when Tori yanked his arm behind his back, twisting it until he dropped to his knees with another curse of pain. He hissed loudly, fur growing on his face, and she yanked viciously on his arm.

"If you shift, I'll break it, I swear to fucking God," she snarled.

He sucked in a large gulp of air. "Let go of me, you fucking bitch!"

She yanked his arm again, relishing the sound of his high-pitched squeal. "Call me bitch one more time, friend."

He moaned with pain, his body shuddering as he stared at her. "Let me go."

"In a minute," she said. "But first, you're going to apologize to me, and you'll make it fucking sincere, or I really will break your goddamn arm, you useless twat of a shifter."

He cried out when she pulled on his arm again. Sweat sliding down his forehead, he said, "Okay, okay, I'm sorry."

"Try the fuck again," she said and yanked mercilessly on his arm.

He hissed out another expletive before sucking in a harsh breath. His eyes locked onto hers, and he said, "I'm sorry. I was an asshole and shouldn't have said what I said."

"And…" she gave his arm another tug.

He squealed, and she kept the grin off her face when tears leaked down his face. "I don't know what you want me to say!"

"Think harder about what you did to me," she said.

Panting and moaning, he stared wild-eyed at her, his pupils dark slits. "I… I shouldn't have…." Understanding dawned in his gaze. "I shouldn't have touched you without your permission."

"Bing-fucking-o," she said. "Top of the class for you. Good boy. She released his arm and stepped back, watching as he rubbed it before staggering to his feet. "Go home, good boy."

He snarled at her, and she sighed. Fuck, he really was going to make her break his bones, all because of male pride. His body started to swell, and she said, "You don't want to do this. I will hurt you."

He stared at her, and she returned his gaze with calm confidence. After a moment, he deflated and turned to leave, still rubbing his arm. He chuffed in surprise, and she followed his gaze, dismay washing over her when she saw Judd standing at the hallway entrance.

Shock covered his features, and he paid no attention to the

tiger shifter when the man pushed past him and disappeared into the bar.

"What the fuck?" Judd said.

"Oh, like, hey, big guy," she said. "You ready to call it a night? It's been such a long shift, am I right?"

He strode down the hall, the floor shaking minutely with every step, to stand before her. "Don't do that."

She pasted a smile on her face. "Don't do what, big guy?"

"Don't use that voice. Don't pretend to be...." Judd looked her up and down, "whatever the fuck this is."

Exhaustion seeping into every bone, she sighed and said, "My shift's over. Good night, Judd."

"Your shift's over?" Judd stared wild-eyed at her. "I just watched you put a fucking tiger shifter on his knees and make him blubber like a baby, and all you have to say is my shift's over?"

"Yes," she said.

"What the fuck, Tori? Who are you? Why are you hiding who you really are behind this fake dumb bunny routine?"

"It's none of your business," she said. "Get out of my way."

She pushed past him but stopped when he said, "What do you think Porter and the others will say when I tell them you're faking the dumb bunny routine?"

Her back stiff, she returned to him. He swallowed hard at the look on her face as she stepped so close her breasts brushed against his chest. "Tori-girl, you -"

She reached up and bopped him lightly on the nose before smiling at him and, laying her Valley girl accent on thick, said, "Like, who would ever believe you, big guy?"

She stood on her tiptoes and brushed her mouth against his. She shouldn't have, but her fucking bunny was all riled up from her encounter with the tiger shifter. She had to touch Judd. She needed to know what his lips felt like against hers.

"Tori," he breathed against her mouth, his voice filled with need.

He gripped her hips, pulling her up against him, and her bunny practically salivated when she felt the hard press of his erection against her belly. She placed her mouth at his ear and, hating herself, said, "If you tell anyone what you just saw, I'll kill you."

His hands tightened and then loosened on her hips before falling away. She stepped back as Carmen stuck her head into the hallway. "There you two are. Porter's locked the doors. Tori, can you help me cash out? I think I fucked up something because my totals aren't matching."

Tori turned and smiled at the pretty capybara shifter. "Like, of course, I can help you, gorgeous."

"Thanks, Tori. You're a lifesaver," Carmen said.

Tori hooked her arm around Carmen's. "Okay, but, like, a red lifesaver, right? Everyone knows they're the best ones."

Carmen laughed, and Tori risked one final look over her shoulder at Judd as they left the hallway. She expected to see fear, maybe even anger, on his face. Instead, a lust so deep it seemed etched permanently into his skin covered his face, and her stupid pussy immediately soaked her underwear.

Ignoring her urge to return to him and ride him like a mechanical bull, she followed Carmen into the bar.

CHAPTER 4

"**Y**ou're my best girl, Lindy-Lou. Yes, you are. You're Daddy's best girl. Do you want another piece of bacon? Come get your bacon, Linda."

The little Pomeranian danced around his feet, and grinning widely, Judd dropped a piece of bacon. She snatched it from the air and chomped it down before barking at him for more.

"No barking, sweetpea. That's your third piece of bacon already."

Linda sat at his feet, her little face so hopeful, he couldn't resist. He gave her a final piece of bacon before wiping his hands on the dishtowel and carrying his plate into the living room. He sat on the couch and unmuted the TV.

The local weatherman pointed to the green screen in front of him that showed their city covered with swirls of blue. "Folks, what you see here is a truly astonishing act of nature. Occurring only every dozen years or so, the Solum Winds have returned as of early yesterday morning. Thanks to climate change, scientists predict this may be the last time we experience Solum Winds this powerful. Now, these winds can drop the temperature by as much as fifteen degrees, so make sure you're bundling up when you're outdoors."

The screen switched to the anchors, and as they bantered with the weatherman, Judd turned the volume to low and dug into his meal. Linda sat docilely at his feet, not quite begging, but definitely giving him the 'if you love me, you'll give me more bacon' look she had perfected over the last eight years.

"Too much bacon isn't good for you, sweetpea," Judd said. "I gotta keep my girl healthy, right?"

He ate a few forkfuls of steamed vegetables, giving Linda some cauliflower and broccoli, which she chewed down with as much enthusiasm as she did the bacon. There was a knock on the front door, and Hudson's voice boomed, "Yo, Judd. You decent?"

"I'm in the living room," he called as Linda took off for the front door with a high-pitched bark that annoyed Judd's bear.

Linda's barking turned to whines of happiness. Judd rolled his eyes when Hudson said from the hallway, "You decent?"

"I'm eating dinner," Judd said. "Yes, I'm fucking decent."

Hudson stepped into the room. He held Linda in one meaty hand, and the little dog looked even tinier than her six pounds when next to the polar bear shifter. She panted happily, climbing Hudson's chest and licking at his face when he sat in the chair beside the couch.

"One time, you walked in on me naked," Judd said. "One fucking time, and you'll never let me forget it."

"I'm the one who had to stare at your naked fucking ass," Hudson said.

"I'll have you know the ladies love my naked fucking ass," Judd said.

"Uh-huh." Hudson shifted in the chair, making it creak a little under his weight.

"You want something to eat?" Judd asked. "There's plenty left."

"Nah, I'm good. Rosalie and I ate before she dropped me off here. Thanks again for the ride to work. My truck won't start again, and Rosalie needs hers tonight."

"You need to buy a new one. Yours is a piece of shit," Judd said.

"Yeah, I know." Hudson held Linda against his chest and petted her head. "But it costs money, and with Rosalie only working part-time while she goes to school, it's not in the budget."

Judd sat back in his chair. "When will you quit the bar and work full-time for Burke, King, and Frost Security? They're desperate for employees, and I know Mal and Kat have offered you a full-time position more than once. You'll make a fuck of a lot more money working for them than as a bartender."

Hudson shrugged. "Mal is Porter's brother. I don't want to cause a wedge between them if I quit the bar to work for Mal."

Judd ate the last of his vegetables. "You won't. Porter's a good guy, and he knows how it is. You're wasting your talents being the bar."

"Beating people up isn't exactly a talent," Hudson said.

"No, but keeping people safe is, and you know you're fucking good at that," Judd said. "Hell, they're so desperate for people that Bishop even asked me if I wanted a job. He said they've taken on a bunch of new corporate clients thanks to some lizard shifter, and they're struggling to keep up."

"So, why aren't you taking him up on it?" Hudson said.

Judd shrugged. "What do I need extra money for? Besides, I like being a bouncer."

"Do you? Or do you just want to be around Tori?"

"That isn't it," Judd said.

"Right," Hudson said.

Judd finished off his food and set his plate on the coffee table. "Speaking of Tori… you notice anything different about her lately?"

"What do you mean?" Hudson set Linda down, and the dog scampered out of the room.

"I mean, has she been acting differently around you?"

"Nope, she's the same airhead she always is," Hudson said.

Judd's bear growled at him, and Hudson cocked one blond eyebrow. "Why are you asking me this?"

Linda returned carrying her favourite toy - a fuzzy rat that squeaked - and she stood on her hind legs, resting her front legs on Hudson's shin and honking the toy at him until he plucked it from her mouth and tossed it across the room.

She chased after it, grabbing it and shaking it viciously before returning to Hudson and honking the toy at him a second time.

As Hudson threw it again, Judd said, "She's faking the dumb bunny thing."

"Why?" Hudson said.

"I dunno, but last night, a tiger shifter tried to manhandle her in the hallway outside the bathrooms, and she handed him his ass. I mean, she had him on his knees, fucking crying for mercy. And she sounded different."

"Different, how?"

"She sounded… normal. I mean, not that she doesn't sound normal now, but you know how she has that high-pitched thing going on when she talks, and every other fucking word out of her mouth is like?"

"I'm aware," Hudson said before tossing Linda's toy a third time.

"That was gone. Her voice was a lot lower and… different," Judd said. He hoped like hell Hudson didn't glance at his lap. Hudson could smell his lust, but he didn't need to see Judd's erection just from thinking about Tori's other voice.

Christ, what it wouldn't do to him to hear that voice whispering in his ear.

You did, remember? When she threatened to kill you.

Yeah, he did. And how fucked up was it that Tori threatening to kill him nearly made his dick come busting through his jeans?

"Hey, did you hear me?" Hudson said.

Judd forced himself to pay attention to Hudson. "No, sorry."

"I said I find it a little hard to believe that Tori took down a tiger shifter," Hudson said.

"She did. I saw it with my own eyes. And then she threatened to kill me if I told anyone about the real her."

Hudson paused with Linda's toy in her hand. She barked impatiently, and he gave it another toss, watching as her paws scrabbled on the wood when she took off after it. "Tori threatened to kill you."

"She did."

"Maybe she was drunk or on drugs last night," Hudson said.

"She doesn't do either," Judd said.

"How do you know? You ever hang out with her outside of work?" Hudson asked.

"No, but… look, all I'm saying is that she's faking the dumb bunny thing. Maybe she does it to get more tips? You know that half the assholes in the bar give her bigger tips the more skin she shows and the dumber she acts."

Hudson rolled his eyes. "Yeah, that's true. But I saw her outside work once, and she acted exactly like she does at the bar. Ditzy as hell."

"I'm telling you, it's a lie. She's faking who she really is," Judd said.

Hudson studied him before nodding. "I believe you."

"Thanks, man," Judd said.

"I won't mention it to Tori, though. I'd be fucking embarrassed to be your friend if a bunny killed you. You're a black bear shifter, for fuck's sake."

"Fuck you," Judd said with a grin.

Hudson gave him another of those rare grins in return. "Fuck you too, buddy. Fuck you too."

"Evening, big guy. How was your day?"

Judd turned away from his post at the door to study Tori. Today, she wore a Bud's tank top that dipped low in the front, showing off a generous amount of her tiny cleavage, and her short skirt was glued to her like a second skin.

"Still pretending like I don't know the real you, huh?" he said.

She just shrugged before cocking her head at him. "You're looking, like, so handsome today."

"Don't flirt with me in that voice," he said.

Her teasing smile disappeared, and she studied the bar around them. It was loud and busy tonight, but she stepped closer anyway and lowered her voice so only he could hear her. "Look, I get you're pissed because I'm not the ditzy bunny you prefer, but -"

"I don't prefer the ditzy bunny, and that's not why I'm pissed," he growled. "I'm pissed because you've lied to me for years, Tori. I thought we were friends."

"Friends?" She scoffed, crossing her arms over her tiny chest. "What exactly makes us friends, Judd? Is it you staring at my ass night after night or me lusting after your dick night after night that makes us friends? Or is it how we never talk outside of this fucking bar? Or maybe it's all the times we haven't bothered to learn anything about each other beyond the goddamn basics?"

He flushed, shame washing over him. "Okay, fine, you're right. I shouldn't have said that, but it doesn't negate that you've been lying to all of us. Why are you lying about who you are?"

"Like I said last night, it's none of your business."

"You also threatened to kill me last night."

"I did," she said.

He stared at her, feeling that old familiar lust rolling over him like fog from the sea. "You meant it."

"I did," she said.

"Christ, I want to fuck you so bad right now," he said.

Her smile lit up her entire face, and his cock pressed against his jeans when she glanced at his dick. "Ditto, big guy."

He blew out his breath. "Fuck, woman. You're gonna be the death of me."

"I want tickets to that show. I've never seen a bunny shifter take down a bear shifter before."

Alfie had joined them, and Tori's face immediately changed to her dumb bunny look. She turned to Alfie and patted his chest - Judd's bear growled in jealousy - before giggling. "Little old me couldn't harm a fly. You know that, Alfie. Judd was being a big silly head."

She smiled at Judd. "Isn't that right, Juddie-pie?"

"Yeah," he grunted.

With another grin, Tori walked away. The door opened, and a hedgehog shifter and giraffe shifter stepped inside, nodding to Judd and Alfie before they made their way to one of the empty booths.

"You okay?" Alfie asked.

"Fine," Judd said. "Excuse me."

He walked away, following the scent of bunny to the pretty shifter sitting at one of the high tables and talking to a beaver shifter. Her eyes lit up when she saw him, and she slid off her seat, bouncing over and throwing her arms around him. "Judd! Hey, handsome!"

"Hi, Lori. It's been a long time since you've been in," he said.

"Oh, I know, right?" she said. "I moved last year to Stony Creek, and I'm here visiting my parents for a few days. Figured I'd hit my old hangout."

"Are you and Tori getting together?" he asked.

A couple of years ago, she and Tori had been good friends. If anyone knew about her secret life, it would be Lori, right?

"Oh, like, no, probably not. We kind of lost touch after I moved." Lori giggled again as she retook her seat. The beaver shifter had wandered off as soon as Judd approached, but Lori didn't seem upset. "I'm, like, so bad at keeping in touch with people if they're not directly on my radar."

"Right," Judd said.

"How've you been?" Lori asked.

"Good. So, uh, hey, you and Tori used to be pretty close, right?"

"Oh, the closest!" Lori said. "We hung out together all the time."

"Cool. So, you've been to her house?" Judd said.

Lori blinked at him, curling her hand around her glass. "Once or twice, but we usually met at my place. Tori said it was easier."

"And you've met her children?"

"Yeah, I've…." Lori stared at him. "Well, no, I didn't meet her kits."

"Your kids never played with hers?" Judd asked.

"No, her kits are older than mine," Lori said.

"Still, it seems weird, doesn't it?"

Lori shrugged, taking a drink of beer as she scanned the bar. She was growing bored of the conversation. Judd could see it on her face and smell it on her scent. Before he lost her attention completely, he said, "You didn't see the kids when you were at her place?"

"No, she said they were at their dad's. But she had pictures of them. Why?" Lori asked.

"Just wondering. It's weird that no one's ever met her kids," Judd said.

"Well, I mean, we were friends, but we weren't that type of friends," Lori said.

"What do you mean?" Judd asked. "You were best friends, weren't you?"

Lori sipped at her beer. "A girl like Tori doesn't really have, like, a best friend. I liked her a lot, and she was super fun to hang out with, but, like, we didn't talk about any deep stuff, you know? There isn't a lot going on in that brain of hers."

Judd's bear growled, and Lori shook her head. "I'm not being mean, just truthful. Tori's a nice girl, just not very bright."

She suddenly let out a squeal that made Judd and his bear wince before she waved wildly at an otter shifter across the bar. "Oh my God, it's Bethany! I gotta say hi to her. Bye, Judd!"

She grabbed her beer and bounced her way across the bar. Judd headed to the bar, leaning against it and studying the room. Despite how busy it was, the bar patrons had been surprisingly well-behaved. Hudson finished pouring a beer and handed it to a deer shifter, ringing through the sale and tossing the change into the tip jar. He joined Judd, his big hands resting on the bar.

"So, any luck?"

"What do you mean?"

"In getting Tori to confess to being a secret scientist or brain surgeon, or whatever the fuck she is."

"No," Judd said. He eyed the room again, his gaze swinging to the door when it opened. A shifter ducked inside, and Judd glanced at Hudson. "Shit, is that…?"

"Briggs?" Hudson came out from behind the bar as the big shifter approached them. "Holy fuck, what are you doing here?"

Judd studied Briggs as he and Hudson embraced. Like Hudson, he was a polar bear shifter and just as big. He was well over seven feet tall and heavily muscled, but where Hudson had hair so blond it was nearly white, Briggs's hair was a rich, dark brown. He clapped Hudson on the back before grinning at him. "Hey, man, how are you?"

"I'm good. You remember Judd?"

Judd held out his hand. He'd met Briggs once or twice when he and Hudson worked construction in Canada. Judd had gone home with Hudson to Alaska a few times on their holidays, and they'd almost always gone for a beer with Briggs.

Briggs shook it firmly. "Good to see you again, Judd."

"You too. You come to the big city for a holiday?"

Briggs shrugged. "Not exactly."

"What do you mean?" Hudson asked.

"I'm living here now. Moved here last weekend."

"Like fuck you are," Hudson said. "You hate the city. There was a reason you never left Wellington."

"People change," Briggs said.

"I talked to my parents last night," Hudson said. "They didn't say anything about you moving here."

"Not a lot of folks back home know," Briggs said.

Judd was curious to know why, but like most polar bear shifters, Briggs didn't say a lot, and Judd knew Hudson well enough to know he wouldn't ask Briggs either.

"Anyway, I thought I'd pop into the bar and say hello."

"It's good to see you," Hudson said. "You working construction here in the city?"

"I haven't found work yet," Briggs said as Porter approached them.

"Porter, this is an old friend Briggs. Briggs, this is my boss, Porter," Hudson said.

"Nice to meet you." Porter shook his hand. "I didn't mean to eavesdrop, but are you looking for work?"

"I am," Briggs said.

Porter looked him up and down before pointing to a booth where his brother Mal, a dark-haired wolf-shifter, sat with his mate, a tiny brunette human named Willow. One of Mal's business partners, a grizzly shifter named Bishop, sat across from them next to his human mate, Ava. "My brother, Mal, co-owns a security firm, and they're looking for employees. Hudson does some part-time work for them, although I imagine he'll be quitting here and going full-time any day now."

Hudson chuffed in surprise, and Porter grinned at him. "Don't look so surprised. Hell, Mal, Bishop, and Kat have been bugging me to come up with some reason to fire you so they can hire you full-time."

"I wouldn't leave you without a bartender," Hudson said.

Porter clapped him on the back. "I appreciate that, man, but you gotta do what's right for you. Give me a couple of weeks to find your replacement is all I'm asking."

He turned back to Briggs. "I can introduce you to Mal and Bishop right now if you'd like."

Briggs glanced at Hudson before nodding. "I'd appreciate that."

"Great, come with me." Porter led Briggs toward the booth.

CHAPTER 5

"Hey there, handsome. You mind if I take this?" Tori pointed to the giant polar bear shifter's empty plate.

"Go ahead. Thank you." His gaze drifted over her, and she could smell his faint lust. That should have gotten her bunny excited, but apparently, the only bear - the only *shifter* - her rabbit was interested in now was Judd.

Our hoo-haw's gonna dry up! Get it together and be the whore I know you are, she snapped at her rabbit.

Her rabbit pouted and turned away. Great. Now she was getting the silent treatment.

Tori plastered a smile on her face as she took the polar bear's plate. He was sitting at the bar, and typically one of the bartenders cleared the plates, but both Hudson and their part-time bartender Mila were dealing with customers at the far end of the bar.

Plus, she'd seen the big polar bear when he came into the bar a few hours ago - he was hard to miss - and she'd noticed him talking to Judd. That automatically piqued her interest in the polar bear.

"So, are you friends with Judd?" She kept her face open

and sweet. Her sudden urge to know everything she could about Judd, including who his friends were, was annoying as fuck.

"Not really. Met him a couple of times." The shifter held out his hand. "Briggs."

"I'm Tori. It's, like, so nice to meet you." She shook his hand, annoyed all over again that her rabbit didn't even stir. Briggs was a damn fine specimen of a shifter with thick dark hair, pretty blue eyes, and a goddamn stellar body. She should have been figuring out how to get him into her bed. Instead, she was picking his brain about Judd.

"So, how do you know Judd?"

Briggs's gaze assessed her coolly, and it took everything she had not to flush. Christ, she was acting like a fool. He sipped his beer and said, "I know Hudson. Met Judd through him."

"Oh, that's, like, so cool," she said.

Briggs stared at her again. She had a feeling he could see right through the dumb bunny act, and apprehension made her skin tight. Shit, was he one of Francis's goons?

Get it together. He just said he was friends with Hudson. You're being paranoid.

Maybe. Maybe not. Either way, it was time to fucking leave.

She smiled at Briggs and turned away, stopping when he wrapped one hand around her forearm. She turned back, cocking her hip out and giving him her best dumb bunny smile as he released her. "You need something else, handsome?"

"That fox shifter at the end of the bar has been staring at you for the last two hours. Make sure someone walks you to your car when your shift's over."

She leaned back to study the fox shifter sitting at the far

end of the bar. He stared at the television screen behind the bar, his hand wrapped around a half-full beer mug.

"He seems pretty occupied with the game," she said.

"He's not," Briggs said. "Watch your back, little bunny."

She looked a final time at the fox, taking in his stiff posture and how he held his beer mug just a little too tightly. After about ten seconds, he glanced her way, his eyes widening slightly before he nodded to her.

She smiled at him, watching him for another few seconds once he returned his gaze to the television before giving her attention to Briggs again. "Thanks, I will."

He nodded and drank some beer just as a scream of outrage echoed through the bar. Tori turned, rolling her eyes when the wolf shifter slid out from the booth and glared at the lion shifter who stood in front of a pretty blonde woman. The front of her dress dripped with beer, turning the light pink material to a dark rose colour.

"You did that on purpose!" The woman shouted as the wolf shifter shoved the lion shifter in the back.

The lion shifter turned with a snarl, baring his teeth at the wolf. "It was an accident. I tripped and lost my grip on my drink."

"Like fuck, it was," the woman said. "He tried to hit on me when I came out of the bathroom and is pissed that I blew him off."

"You hit on my mate?" The wolf shifter's body swelled.

"Oh shit," Tori said.

Briggs slid off his stool and stepped in front of her, and while she appreciated the chivalry, she slipped out from behind him and scanned the bar for Judd and Alfie.

"Knock it off!" Judd was already pushing his way through the crowd of shifters. "Both of you just calm the fuck down before… oh, are you fucking kidding me?"

Judd's exasperated growl was lost beneath the wolf's howl as he shifted fully and leaped at the lion shifter. The lion shifter went down in a tangle of limbs and curses before shifting to his lion form. Snarling and growling, they rolled across the floor, tearing at each other with their fangs.

With another annoyed growl, Judd shifted to his bear, his clothes landing in tatters around him as Alfie, already in his leopard form, joined him.

Judd pulled the wolf shifter off the lion with a low roar, dragging him back nearly five feet before releasing him. He moved in front of the wolf shifter, rising to his back feet and letting loose with another roar when the wolf tried to duck around him.

The wolf backed away. He snarled and growled but didn't attempt to push past Judd as Alfie hissed at the lion shifter behind them.

With a low pop, Judd shifted back to his human form. He glared at the wolf. "Shift, you asshole."

The wolf shifted, ignoring the catcalls of other patrons as they stared at his and Judd's naked bodies. "That asshole hit on my mate."

"Not my fucking problem," Judd snapped. "Jesus Christ, Derek, you know you can't fucking shift in here and go after someone like that. What the fuck has gotten into you tonight?"

"He dumped his beer on Sharon!" Derek snarled.

"It was an accident. I saw the lion trip," Judd said.

He turned to the wolf's mate. "Sharon, you know it was an accident."

She sniffed, pulling at her wet dress. "He ruined my dress."

Alfie and the lion shifter returned to their human forms,

the lion pushing Alfie away when Alfie tried to take his arm. "It was an accident. Keep your mate under control before I - "

"You shut your fucking mouth," Judd barked at him. He turned back to Derek. "Go home, Derek, before I ban you from the bar for a month."

"I didn't do anything!" Derek growled.

"You fucking attacked another shifter, and I had to shift to stop you," Judd said.

Derek rubbed at his mouth. "Christ. I've had too much to drink."

"Yeah, you have. So get Sharon to take you home," Judd said.

Derek nodded. "Sorry, man."

"Get home safe, you two." Judd clapped the wolf shifter on the back as Sharon joined them and took Derek's hand.

Sharon handed Derek her sweater, and he wrapped it around his waist before following her out the door. The crowd slowly dispersed, a buzz of disappointment in the air that the fight had ended so soon.

Judd walked over to the lion shifter. "You got extra clothes in your car, or do you need the box?"

The box was actually a large plastic bin that Porter kept behind the bar. It was filled with generic shorts and t-shirts in different sizes for both men and women.

"I need the box," the lion shifter said.

Hudson was already bringing the bin over, and he dropped it in front of the lion shifter before tossing jeans to Alfie and Judd. "I grabbed these from your lockers."

"Thanks, Hudson." Judd unfolded his jeans as the lion shifter, not the least bit self-conscious about his nudity, squatted and rummaged through the bin.

As Judd pulled on his jeans, Tori forced her gaze upward. Her bunny thumped in anger, the sound echoing in Tori's head, but she ignored her rabbit's demands. Not that she hadn't seen Judd's dick a time or two, it was nearly impossible not to if he was forced to shift while at work, but she didn't deliberately look at his dick, despite how much her rabbit begged her to. The man deserved some privacy.

But it's so pretty. I wanna see it. Please?

Her bunny was whining like a distraught toddler.

The lion shifter had pulled on a t-shirt and shorts, and Alfie walked him to the door as Judd and Hudson headed toward the bar. Carmen joined Tori and Briggs, studying Judd's naked chest with appreciation. She nudged Tori. "Christ, Judd's body is something else, huh?"

As Hudson tossed the bin behind the bar and Briggs returned to his barstool, Carmen smiled at Judd, one hand caressing his upper arm. "Nice work, Judd."

Tori itched to slap Carmen's hand away, but she clenched the empty plate instead.

"Fucking Derek," Judd said. Irritation blew off him in hot waves. "I just put in two new barbells last night."

Tori started to laugh, remembering just in time to do her fake shitty giggle. Porter, who had joined them, also snorted laughter. Even Hudson cracked a smile as Briggs stared at them politely, and Carmen said, "What? What's so funny?"

Porter clapped Judd on the back. "I keep telling you, man, the last thing a bouncer at a shifter bar needs is nipple rings."

"They're not rings, they're barbells, and I like them," Judd said stubbornly.

"You have nipple piercings?" Carmen studied Judd's chest. "You don't seem the type."

Porter laughed again. "I know, right? He loses them almost every night he works too. How many replacement barbells have you had to buy, buddy?"

"I buy them in bulk," Judd said.

Tori giggled, ignoring Judd's 'I know that's not your real laugh' look, before saying, "Like, poor Judd, he should probably buy stock in barbells. I swear I've swept up ten pairs in the last month alone."

"I assume you want to go to the staff room and put new ones in?" Porter said with a grin.

"Yeah," Judd said. "They'll heal over if I don't, and if I go in one more time to get my nipples re-pierced, my piercer Ally's gonna bust my balls more than you are right now."

Porter laughed so hard his face turned red. "Go take your break, buddy. You deserve it."

"Do you need help putting the new ones in?" Carmen smiled at Judd, her hand reaching out to linger on his bicep again.

Judd studied her, and when it looked like he might say yes, Tori's bunny thumped so hard and loud that Tori staggered back.

"You okay?" Briggs steadied her with one big hand. He arched one thick eyebrow when Judd made a low growl at him.

"Fine," Tori said as Briggs released her arm. "Hey, Porter, you okay with me taking my break now too?"

"Sure," Porter said. "I'll take that plate to the kitchen for you."

He took the plate and walked away, and Tori gave Carmen a stiff smile. "I'm happy to help Judd."

"Sure, okay," Carmen said with obvious disappointment.

"Ready, big guy?" Tori asked.

Judd nodded and followed her down the back hallway past Porter's office. She punched in the key code to the staff room and stepped inside. Judd closed the door behind them, and Tori immediately slipped off her heels before padding over to the small fridge and opening it.

The staff room was minuscule, with just enough room for a row of lockers for the staff, a small counter with a row of cupboards above it that housed a few glasses, plates, and cutlery, the fridge, and a love seat. She grabbed an apple from her lunch bag and leaned against the counter, watching Judd as he opened his locker and brought out a leather bag. He rummaged through it, and she ate a few bites of her apple, studying Judd's ass.

He pulled two new barbells from the bag and grabbed a t-shirt from his locker before closing it and joining her at the counter. He set his t-shirt and one of the barbells on the counter.

"Do you need help?" she asked. Christ, it was a relief to use her normal voice.

He shook his head. "I've been putting these in by myself for the last five years. It's not exactly rocket science."

She ignored both her and her bunny's disappointment. So, she didn't get to touch Judd, so fucking what? It's not like Carmen got to touch him either.

She ate the rest of her apple, watching Judd slide the barbell into his left nipple and screw on the ball before grabbing the other barbell.

Feeling like a pervert, she tossed her apple core in the garbage and grabbed her phone from her locker, scrolling through her emails. Not that she had any that weren't spam. Her family had long given up trying to communicate with her, and she didn't make real friends. Ever.

Judd muttered a curse, and she looked up to see him still fumbling with the barbell. She tossed her phone back in the locker and joined him at the counter. "What's wrong?"

"I can't get the fucking right one in," he said in annoyance.

She laughed. "So, it is rocket science, and you do need my help, is what I'm hearing."

He growled at her, and she gave him a teasing grin. "Do you want my help, or do you want to go back to Ally for another piercing?"

He sighed and handed the barbell to her. Her bunny practically doing cartwheels, she moved closer and studied his perfect flat nipple before easing the barbell into the hole. He sucked in a breath, and she stopped, looking up at him. "Sorry, does this hurt?"

He shook his head, his lips tight and his dark eyes nearly black in the light. "No. Keep going."

She pushed, feeling a tiny bit of resistance. "I think it's already started healing over."

"Just push it through," he said.

Feeling weirdly squeamish, she pushed it through with a firm movement, smiling with relief when the bar popped through on the other side of his nipple. She screwed on the ball and then patted his chest. "There, all... Judd?"

"Yeah?" Judd's hands were gripping her hips.

She let her hand roam across his perfect chest, toying with the light layer of hair that covered it. "You're touching me."

"You're touching me, too," he said.

She looked up, catching her breath at the lust on Judd's face. She wet her bottom lip, and Judd's low groan when he caught sight of her tongue sent a wave of desire through her.

"We shouldn't," she whispered.

"Probably not," he said and kissed her.

CHAPTER 6

Tori's lips were as soft as he'd dreamed they were. Judd pulled her closer, her slender body pressing against his as he deepened the kiss. She parted her lips for him. Her soft moan when he touched his tongue delicately against hers made his bear growl happily.

Her tiny hands roamed across his naked back, tracing the large muscles until he ground his erection against her abdomen. He grunted in annoyance - he wanted to feel her pussy against his dick - and picked her up, planting her on top of the counter and pushing between her thighs.

She laughed, a low sound that was a thousand times hotter than that fake-ass giggle she did, and wrapped her thighs around his waist, urging him closer. He didn't need a second invitation. He crowded close, pressing his aching dick against her core.

She moaned again, and when she rubbed her small breasts against his chest, he immediately cupped one, squeezing gently before rubbing his thumb over her nipple. She kissed him hard, exploring every inch of his mouth with her tongue as her hands roamed through his dark hair.

She arched encouragingly when he squeezed her breast again, and he slipped his hand under her tank top. He wanted to feel her hard nipple directly against his palm, wanted to -

"Hey! No sex in the staff room, you two."

His bear snarled at Hudson's voice as Judd yanked his hand from under Tori's shirt. He wanted to shift. He wanted to release his bear so he could kick his best friend's ass for interrupting.

"Keep your cool, big guy." Tori's hand rubbed across his cheek, smoothing down his beard. "He's right."

Judd stepped back and lifted Tori off the counter, setting her down with infinite care before turning and glaring at Hudson. He adjusted his dick with a grimace. "What are you doing in here?"

"It's the staff room. I'm on my break." Hudson sniffed in Judd's direction before grinning. "You can try to kick my ass, but you know I'll win the fight."

Judd growled at him, and Hudson's grin widened. "It's been a long time since we had a good fight, old friend. You've forgotten what happened the last time."

"I seem to remember you had plenty of wounds to lick," Judd said.

Hudson's grin turned to a laugh. "And you had three broken ribs and a nearly ruptured spleen."

"You two, like, seriously got into a fight?" Tori's fake voice was back, and Judd's bear cringed at the sound. She grabbed a bottle of water from the fridge and took a long drink before handing it to Judd. "You're best friends."

Hudson shrugged. "We were bored."

Tori stared at him as Judd drank a few swallows of water. "Oh, I, like, need to hear that story."

"We were working construction in this shitty ass tiny

town in northern Alberta. There was fuck all to do," Judd said.

"So, you fought your best friend? A giant polar bear shifter," Tori said.

Judd just shrugged and handed her the water bottle before pulling his t-shirt over his head. "I wanted to see if I could take him down."

"Which you couldn't," Hudson said.

"I almost did," Judd said. "Until you pussied out on me and refused to keep fighting."

Hudson snorted and said to Tori, "Both his eyes had swelled completely shut. Fighting him at that point was like taking candy from a baby."

Tori did her fake giggle before patting Judd's shoulder and heading toward the door, where she slipped into her heels. "Like, you bear boys are sooo silly. See you later, handsome."

She left the staff room as Hudson crossed to the fridge and took out a lunch bag roughly the size of a small suitcase. "You shouldn't be making out with Tori at work."

"Says the guy who made out with his mate in our boss's office," Judd said.

Hudson sank into the small love seat, making the cushions nearly sag to the floor. "You got me there."

Judd sighed and leaned against the counter. "I didn't mean for it to happen."

Hudson opened his lunch bag and rummaged through it. "She tell you why she's using that fake voice and shit, yet?"

"No, and I doubt she will," Judd said.

Hudson, with a double-decker roast beef sandwich in one hand, turned to stare at him. "She's hiding who she is for a reason, and we both know that reason isn't good. She's trouble, Judd. You gotta stay away from her."

"Yeah, I know."

"Okay, Haruto," Tori pushed past the swinging door that led into the kitchen, "the customers are gone, the front doors are locked, and it's just, like, you and me left. You ready to… Haruto, what's wrong?"

Tori studied Haruto's small and compact body as he paced back and forth in front of the industrial stove, texting on his phone.

Haruto had been the head cook at Bud's Bar for the last fifteen years. The otter shifter was an affable and friendly guy who spent most of his breaks in the staff room, showing off pictures of his kids.

She could smell his anxiety, and she joined him by the stove. "Is Alicia okay?"

"She's fine," Haruto said. "But our youngest, Kaito, has been in a car accident."

"Shit. Is he okay?" Tori asked.

"They've taken him to the hospital. He has a broken leg and maybe some internal injuries." He smacked his leg in frustration. "He's not a shifter. He's human like Alicia. He doesn't heal like we… Alicia's at the hospital, alone and scared and…."

He took a deep shuddering breath as Tori put her arm around his narrow shoulders. "Go, Haruto."

"I can't. I still need to take out the garbage and sweep the floor, and it's my turn to lock up," Haruto said.

"I'll do all of that," Tori said. "Like, you have to go, honey. Alicia needs you."

"Judd will have my head if I leave you here alone to lock up," Haruto said.

"It'll be, like, totally fine. Just go," Tori said. She pushed him toward the back door, handing him his jacket that hung on a hook by the door. "Drive safe, and give Alicia and Kaito my love."

"Tori, are you sure? I could call Judd or Hudson. I'm sure one of them would be happy to come back and help you lock up." Haruto chewed at his bottom lip, and she could smell his anxiety deepen.

"Don't be silly," she said. "My car is parked right by the back door. I'll be fine. Go to your mate, Haruto."

His phone chimed again. "Oh shit, they're taking him into surgery."

"Go!" She pushed him toward the door, and he squeezed her hand distractedly before hurrying out the back door. She stood in the doorway until he drove away before shutting the door and grabbing the broom.

She pushed the broom across the floor with brisk movements. The rest of the night had gone agonizingly slow despite how busy the bar was. She supposed it was because she couldn't wait to get the fuck home and masturbate into a coma. Her little make-out session with Judd in the staff room had her bunny so worked up that Tori could barely concentrate. She'd had to avoid Judd for the rest of the night. Hell, as soon as the bar was closed, she'd hidden in the ladies' room until she was sure he'd left for the night. She would have invited herself back to his place to finish what they'd started if she hadn't.

Why can't we? Her bunny wavered between pouting and actual anger. *We've slept with plenty of guys from the bar, including Porter! C'mon, just once!*

She pushed the broom more firmly. Like most rabbit shifters, controlling her libido was one of her hardest struggles. And yeah, she'd slept with Porter a few years ago, back when he was still only a bartender at the bar and single. While she'd enjoyed it then, she'd had plenty of regrets later.

Story of her life, right?

How would you know? There's a significant chunk of it you can't remember.

She pushed that errant thought out of her head as easily as she pushed the broom across the floor. She'd done what she had to, and there was no point in thinking about it.

She finished sweeping the floor and grabbed her purse before slipping into her jacket. She returned to the kitchen, tied the garbage bag and set it outside by the back door before punching in the security code and locking the back door. She tossed her purse into her car and heaved the garbage bag over her shoulder. She carried it to the dumpster at the far end of the back parking lot and tossed it in before staring at the sky. It was thick with heavy clouds, and snowflakes drifted down.

She stuck out her tongue and caught a few. Her lust had suddenly faded, replaced by an all too familiar sick feeling in her stomach. Ever since Judd had discovered her secret, she'd tried to tell herself it was fine, that it didn't matter. But the truth was that she had a decision to make.

She either had to leave the city or kill Judd.

For a moment, she was so nauseous she nearly vomited. She gripped her stomach and breathed deeply through the worst of it. She couldn't kill Judd, no way, no how, which meant she needed to pack up her shit and move on. Maybe Judd would keep her secret, or maybe he wouldn't, but it was too dangerous for her to stay either way.

You should have left last night.

Yeah, she should have. She'd left the bar last night intending to be in a different city by tonight. Only she couldn't do it. She told herself she was too tired to pack and owed it to Porter to give him two weeks' notice.

She told herself one lie after another because she couldn't admit the truth. She didn't want to leave Judd.

She sighed and started toward her car, slipping a little in the snow. Thank Christ, she'd changed into her boots. She'd be flat on her ass if she still wore her... the thick scent of human drifted to her, and she turned to study the four men standing behind her. The dim light from the bulb by the back door illuminated their faces, revealing a mixture of amusement and disbelief. They were dressed similarly in army fatigues and black knitted hats, and they all carried guns.

Cold survival settled over her like an old friend she hadn't seen in too long.

"This is her?" A blond man looked her up and down. "You're kidding me, right?"

"I'm not." The biggest man, who had dark hair, a cunningly sharp face, and the air of a leader, glanced at the other three. "She's apparently more dangerous than she looks."

The third man snorted. "She weighs, what... ninety pounds soaking wet? I'd break her wrist just by giving it a hard squeeze."

"He wants her brought to him unharmed," the leader said. "He was very clear about that."

"What kind of shifter is she, anyway?" The fourth man had already relaxed, shoving his gun back into the holster at his waist.

"Rabbit," the leader said.

"Jesus Christ," the blond man said. "He sent four of us for a fucking bunny? Is that why he sent humans instead of shifters?"

The leader shrugged. "He said he didn't want to waste shifters on her."

"So, instead, he wastes our time? He's such a fucking wanker," the blond man said.

"You're getting paid, aren't you?" the third man said.

"True, but still... I could have been home watching *The Bachelor.*"

"You and that fucking show," the third man said. "It's rotting your brain."

"Fuck you, Alex," the blond man said.

Alex grabbed his crotch in one gloved hand and thrust it in the blond man's direction. "Anytime, anywhere, Rodney."

"Both of you shut the fuck up," the leader said. He took a couple of steps forward. He still held his gun, but Tori could smell his complacency. "C'mon, lady, you're coming with us."

She gave him a shaky smile. "Like, sorry, guys, but I really need to get home."

The leader shook his head. "Not tonight, sweetheart. Get your ass over here now."

She stayed where she was, letting her body shake and even squeezing out a few tears as her rabbit thumped with excitement. The smell of fox assaulted her nose, and she looked to her right, studying the small red fox who hovered at the corner of the building.

"We don't have all night, lady," Rodney said. With a glance at the others, he trotted forward, and she made a frightened squeak when he wrapped his hand around her arm. "Let's go, bunny rabbit."

She let him drag her forward until they were only a few feet from the others before she dug in her heels. Rodney gave her an impatient look. "Seriously?"

"Do you know why he sent humans and not shifters for me?" she said.

He squeezed her upper arm in a brutal grip. "Why's that, sweetheart?"

"Because he thinks humans are worthless," she said. "He won't give one fuck when I kill you all."

Rodney gaped at her before bursting into loud laughter. "Oh, now that's fucking funny, little baby bunny."

He snorted more laughter, the sound turning to a wail of pain when Tori slammed the heel of her right hand into his nose. It broke with the sound of a gunshot, and he staggered back, his hands cupping his face. He stared in disbelief at the blood pooling in his palms before looking at her.

"You broke my nose, you bitch!" He reached for his gun, his eyes widening when he felt the empty holster.

"Looking for this, handsome?" Tori raised the gun she'd taken from him and shot him in the chest.

CHAPTER 7

R odney staggered and fell, blood splattering across the snow as he landed on his back with a thud.

"Holy fuck," Alex said. "She just shot Rodney. She fucking shot -"

Tori shot Alex in the face, her bunny bouncing with glee when his face exploded in a spray of blood and brains.

She aimed at the fourth man as he stared in slack shock, his hand fumbling for the gun in his holster. "Lady, no, just wait. Okay? Just wait, I wasn't gonna hurt you. I swear to fucking God."

Before she could fire, the leader rammed into her, knocking the gun from her hand and slamming her back up against the dumpster. He wrapped his meaty hand around her throat and lifted her, brutally squeezing as she clawed at his hand.

"You just killed two of my men," he snarled. "He wants you unharmed, but I gotta tell you, sweetheart, I'm not feeling real fucking generous right about now. I'm gonna beat the shit out of you and take the fucking pay cut for it. Do you hear me, little bunny?"

Black spots swarming across her vision, her lungs screeching for oxygen, she kicked him in the nuts. He screamed and dropped her, staggering back with his hands cupped over his crotch as he fell to his knees.

"You bitch," he wheezed.

Choking and gasping, she grabbed the dropped gun and dove around the dumpster as the fourth man fired. Searing pain grazed along her thigh, and her bunny thumped with rage.

"Stop fucking shooting at her!" The leader snarled. "He wants her alive!"

She glanced at her thigh. The bullet had dug a bloody furrow across the outside of her thigh, and blood soaked into her tights.

The fourth man peeked around the dumpster, and she fired the gun at him, narrowly missing him. He cursed and disappeared. "She's got Rodney's gun."

"Tell me something I don't fucking know, asshole," the leader barked.

She set the gun beside her and ripped off her tights, leaving the bottom half crumpled around the top of her boots, before using them to tie a pressure bandage over the wound on her left thigh. She reached for the gun, cursing when she saw the slide was locked back. She was out of ammo.

Fucking Rodney. The lazy asshole couldn't even be bothered to have a full mag.

"How much ammo you got left, sweetheart?" The leader called. "Rodney had a real fucking bad habit of carrying a less than full mag."

"Why don't you come back here, and I'll show you how much ammo I have, dick for brains," she said as she studied the darkness beyond the dumpster. A chain link fence surrounded the bar, and the gate to that chain link fence was on the other end of the parking lot. She eyed the fence before studying her leg. She couldn't climb the fence with her injured leg, at least not before they fucking shot her in the back.

Shift! Her bunny bounced eagerly. *Shift, and I'll get us the fuck out of here.*

I can barely walk on the leg, and you think you can run on it?

Her bunny pouted but knew Tori was right. She was fast in her bunny form but not with a damn bullet wound in her thigh.

"Come on out, sweetheart. Play nice, and I promise to give you a nice juicy carrot."

"I'm allergic to carrots," she hollered. "Why don't you join me, and I'll give you a nice juicy bullet hole to the forehead like I did to your friend."

"Fuck, Rodney's still breathing." The fourth man sounded panicked and overwhelmed. "We gotta get him to a hospital, man. He's still breathing."

"Shut the fuck up," the leader snarled. "We need to grab the bitch bunny and get the fuck out of here before someone calls the fucking cops."

"I ain't going back there," the man said sullenly. "She'll fucking kill me."

Tori stood and put some weight on her left thigh. With her healing abilities, she could probably walk on it, but she couldn't run. Rabbits healed relatively fast, thanks to their metabolism, but they weren't like bears when it came to rapid healing, which was fucking unfortunate for her.

"Bitch, come out right fucking now. I am done playing games," the leader said.

"Fine," she said. "I'm coming out. Don't fucking shoot me."

Holding the empty gun, she limped from behind the dumpster and raised the gun at the leader. "Don't make me shoot you, handsome."

The leader grinned. "Your gun is empty, or you would have shot me already."

She sighed and tossed the gun to the ground. "This is pointless. I can't tell him what he wants to know."

"I don't give a fuck what he wants with you." The leader aimed his gun at her. "Start walking."

She studied him and then his friend, who still crouched next to poor doomed Rodney, that cold survival working overtime to calculate her best chance of killing them both.

"We can't leave Rodney, man," the fourth man said. He had removed his knitted hat and held it to the bleeding wound on Rodney's chest.

"We gotta go," the leader said.

"You sound a little high-pitched there, pal," Tori said. "Your balls still somewhere up around your ribcage?"

Goading him into attacking her was her best option. She was stronger than she looked and fast. Getting his gun from him wasn't beyond the realm of possibilities.

"Fuck you," he said. "Michael, get the fuck over here."

Michael's throat worked compulsively. "John, we can't leave him. He's hurt."

"Yeah, John," Tori said. "Don't be such a dick to your friend."

"I said shut the fuck up!" John snapped. "Don't you fucking run, or I'll shoot you in the back, I swear to God."

He stomped over to Michael and Rodney and yanked Michael to his feet. "We are leaving, asshole."

"Rodney is -" Michael flinched when John shot Rodney in the head.

Her muscles bunching in anticipation and her bunny thumping eagerly, Tori limped silently toward the two of them. She ignored the pain in her thigh as she let her front teeth lengthen.

"There? You fucking happy?" John said. "Does that make you feel -"

He squealed in shock when Tori jumped him head-on, wrapping her legs around his waist, one hand reaching for his gun as she sank her long front teeth into his throat.

"Fuuck!" John roared. He tried to shake her loose as she worked to pry the gun from his hand. His thick, salty blood filled her mouth, and she bit deeper, grinning fiercely at his scream of pain.

He punched her in the ribs with his free hand. She grunted at the excruciating agony but didn't release her grip with her teeth or hand. He howled in pain and punched her twice more in the ribs before landing a blow to her temple. Dazed, she dropped off him, her injured leg giving out on her and sending her into a crumpled heap on the snowy ground.

Michael yanked her to her feet, holding her arms tightly, his garlic breath blowing hot waves across the back of her head as they both faced the bleeding, cursing John.

"What the actual fuck?" John touched his throat and stared at the bright red blood on his hand. "You fucking bit me!"

She spit out a mouthful of his blood. "What's the matter, sweetheart? You don't like it rough?"

He raised the gun. "I am going to shoot you in the fucking face."

"He wants her alive," Michael said.

"I don't fucking care," John said.

Michael's body stiffened behind her as a low growl erupted from the darkness behind John. Fresh adrenaline pumped into Tori's body. She could only see about as well as a human in the dark, but she recognized that growl.

"John," Michael whispered. "John, there's a bear behind you."

John turned slowly as the black bear emerged from the darkness. The bear growled at John, baring his thick sharp teeth before he stood on his back legs. His hand shaking wildly, John raised his gun, and the bear slapped it from his hand like it was a toy.

"Please," John whispered as the front of his pants darkened with urine. "Please, I wasn't gonna hurt her. I wasn't gonna...."

His voice turned to a shriek of fear as the bear sunk his long claws into his shoulders and yanked him forward. He bent his head and tore out John's throat with a low roar. Blood sprayed across the bear's chest, and he roared again as John made a gurgling sound and clutched weakly at his throat.

He died only a few seconds later, and the bear dropped him disinterestedly to the ground before staring at Tori and Michael.

"Fuck me," Michael said and aimed his gun at the bear. Tori elbowed him in the gut, doubling him over as she yanked the weapon from his hand. She turned, shoved Michael back against the dumpster, and shot him twice in the chest.

Michael stared at her, his eyes wide and mouth opening and closing like a fish. He slumped against the dumpster, sliding down to the ground, and dead before he landed on his ass in the snow.

Tori dropped the gun beside him and turned to face the

bear. He chuffed at her before he shifted to his human form with a low pop.

She sucked in a shuddering breath of cold air. "Hello, Judd."

"Holy shit," he said, his gaze wandering over the four dead men. "You're some kind of goddamn assassin."

CHAPTER 8

"I'm not an assassin," Tori said.

Judd's bear growled in warning, and Judd turned to the right, sniffing the air. A fox skittered along the fence, its tail tucked between its legs and its head down before it ran out the gate and disappeared into the darkness.

Judd turned back to Tori. "Like fuck you aren't an assassin. There are four dead men in the parking lot, Tori."

"You killed one of them," she said. "Maybe you're an assassin."

"Tori, wait." He followed her when she limped toward her car. "Christ, wait a minute, would you?"

He took her arm, tugging her to a gentle stop. She turned and looked him up and down, her gaze lingering on his dick. He could smell her lust, and his cock hardened. She made a soft sound of pleasure.

"Tori," he said as she took a step toward him, her nose twitching and desire stamped into her pretty face, "you're injured and -"

She launched herself at him, and he caught her, groaning when she wrapped her slender legs around his waist and rubbed her pussy against his throbbing dick. She kissed him hard, her tongue demanding entrance. He opened his mouth, returning her kiss, his hands squeezing her ass through her short skirt before sliding under it and gripping her ass.

Fuck! She was wearing a thong. He cupped her perfect ass, marveling at the softness of her skin before common sense kicked in.

He pulled his mouth from hers. "Tori, you're hurt and -"

"Judd!" She cupped his face, holding it tight in her hands. "I need you to fuck me right now."

"Tori, we can't."

"Fuck me, Judd," she said and reached between them to grip his dick. She gave him a few firm strokes, and when her thumb rubbed over his tip, common sense abandoned him. He growled and turned to push her up against the cold brick wall of the bar.

He braced her body against the wall before reaching under her skirt and tearing her panties away. He dropped them on the ground as she lifted her skirt around her waist. He reached between her thighs and cupped her pussy. She was soaking wet, and he growled his approval before rubbing her clit with his fingertips.

She moaned, her body arching against his before she knocked his hand away, grabbed his dick again, and guided it to her entrance. "Judd, fuck me right fucking now!"

He thrust forward, his dick sliding into the hottest, tightest pussy he'd ever felt. He pinned her against the wall, his hands gripping her narrow hips as she clutched at his shoulders and met each of his frantic thrusts.

He leaned back, watching his dick slide in and out of her perfect pussy as he growled his pleasure. She moaned his name, her hips rocking back and forth, her breath coming in sharp pants, before she made a low moan and her pussy tightened around his dick. She came hard and silently, her body shaking against his as he wrapped his hands around her thighs, spread her wide, and did his best to fuck her right into the goddamn wall.

She clung to him, her pussy milking his dick, her fingers digging into his back as she took every driving thrust of his cock. He roared in pleasure when his orgasm shot through him and pumped hard and fast into her as he emptied himself into her hot pussy.

He shook against her as he came down from his high, listening to her soft, quick pants in his ear while she stroked his back. He felt the blood-soaked fabric beneath his right hand, and guilt washed over him, replacing the lingering pleasure of his orgasm with ruthless efficiency.

Moving carefully, he pulled out of her and eased her to the ground. She tugged down her skirt as he studied the bloodied remains of her tights tied around her thigh. "Fuck, Tori, I shouldn't have -"

"It's fine," she said. "My ribs hurt worse."

"Jesus," he ran his hand through his hair, "we shouldn't have fucked."

She shrugged. "Yeah, story of my life."

Hurt rolled through him. He'd meant they shouldn't fuck because she was injured, but it was more than clear her injuries weren't why she regretted what they'd just done.

"Why did you come back?" she asked.

"Haruto called me. He was worried about leaving you to lock up alone and asked me to come back. Guess he had every right to be worried."

She sighed. "Okay. Go home, Judd."

"What?" He stared at her.

"Go home," she said.

"There are four dead bodies in the parking lot of our place of employment," Judd said. "We need to call the police."

"You call the police, and I'll be arrested," she said. "Simple as that."

"It was self-defense," Judd said.

She limped her way to her car and opened the door. He caught her arm again before she could slide into the front seat. "Tori, stop."

She shook free of his grip, giving him a look of weariness. "Trust me. The bodies will be gone before dawn. The guy who sent them always cleans up his mess."

"You need to go to the hospital," he said. He studied her thigh, anxiety making his bear pace restlessly.

"It'll heal," she said. "You need to go, Judd. Before more of his people show up."

"Before more of whose people?" he asked. "Tori, what the fuck is going on?"

"I'll explain later," she said. "Go home, and we'll talk tomorrow, okay?"

"Tori -"

"Please, Judd. I've been shot, used as a punching bag, and," she stared down at her jacket covered in blood, "I'm covered in human blood. I want to go home. I need a hot shower and some sleep."

She studied his naked body, and the blood spattered across his chest. "We both need a hot shower."

"I'm calling you first thing in the morning," he said. "If you don't answer, I'll be on your fucking doorstep. Do you understand?"

She nodded and gave him a fragile smile that made his chest tighten. "Go home and put your barbells in, big guy. We'll talk later."

She climbed into her car and drove away without a second glance. He walked slowly to his SUV, grabbed his spare clothes from the trunk, and pulled them on. He tried to ignore his and his bear's unease. Tori said they would talk tomorrow.

So, why did he get the feeling that he would never see her again?

MORE MEN WAITED FOR HER AT HER APARTMENT BUILDING. Three of them in a beige Toyota Camry parked across from the building.

Tori sighed and melted into the darkness of the alley again. She leaned against the wall. Her thigh burned, her ribs ached, and her pussy felt like it had gone a couple of rounds with the biggest dildo in her collection.

Girl, please. Judd's cock was way bigger than your biggest dildo. Fuck, it was beautiful, wasn't it?

Christ, yes. It was magnificent, actually, but it'd also been an epic mistake to fuck him. She closed her eyes, scolding her bunny internally, until the creature thumped with annoyance. When would her libido stop getting her into these messes with men?

Doesn't matter. You'll never see him again, anyway.

Her bunny sat up, her annoyance gone and anxiety taking its place. She didn't like the idea of never seeing Judd again, not at all, but Tori didn't have the time to explain why they couldn't take Judd with them.

She needed to figure out how to get the fuck into her building without Francis's goons seeing her. They were most likely human, but she didn't have it in her to go another round, not even with humans. She was bone-tired, and her ribs were killing her. She hoped they were just bruised and not broken.

She pressed experimentally on them, hissing out a breath before straightening. She needed to get into her apartment, needed the cash and passports hidden beneath the loose floorboard in her bedroom. Returning to her own country was a mistake she didn't intend to make again. Some tiny obscure town in the middle of fucking Europe was her new destination.

She tried to think past the pain in her ribs, her nose twitching when she caught a familiar scent. She moved to the front of the alley, listening to the offkey singing and the stumbling sound of footsteps. When he passed the alley opening, she grabbed his arm and yanked him into the alley, clamping her hand over his mouth when he screamed in surprise.

"Noah, it's me."

The handsome Black man blinked at her, and when recognition lit up his eyes, she dropped her hand from his mouth.

"Tori, how's it going?" He held out his fist, and she bumped it.

"Good." The smell of weed clung to him, as did the faint scent of alcohol. "You just getting home from a party?"

"Fuck yeah," he said. "Cold as shit to be walking, but my fucking Uber never showed. Me and my college fam threw an epic bash, though. It was lit. Cara was there, and she's a fucking snack. She gave me her digits, and we're meeting after class tomorrow. You just gettin' home from work?"

He squinted at her jacket. "Shit, is that blood?"

"No," she said. "Listen, I need you to do me a favour."

"Sure," he said. "You know you're my favourite rabbit shifter. Hey, Cara loves rabbits. You think you can shift and let her pet you?"

"Fuck no," Tori said.

Noah snorted laughter. "Shit, yeah, I guess not. Humans, we're the fucking worst, am I right?"

He raised his fist, and she bumped it again. "I need you to carry me into the building."

"Sure." He slid his backpack off and turned around. "Hop on."

He paused and then laughed. "Hop on... fuck, get it?"

She laughed and winced when it made her rib pain flare to life. "I'll be in my bunny form. I need you to put me in your backpack so no one can see me. You can let me out once we're in our hallway, okay?"

He turned and studied her in the dim light from the street light. After a few seconds, he shrugged. "Yeah, okay."

"Thanks, Noah." She opened his backpack and stuffed her purse on top of a physics textbook and a book titled *A Short History of the Movies*. Noah was a massive movie buff who could quote extensive passages from movies she'd never even heard of. "Turn around."

He blinked at her, and she twirled her fingers. "Turn."

"Right," he said and turned to stare out the mouth of the alley. "You think I have a chance with Cara? She's got a 3.9 GPA."

"You have a 3.8," Tori said as she shrugged off her jacket and tossed it into the dumpster. "She'd be lucky to date you, bud."

"You sound different." Noah glanced over his shoulder at her. "Not as dumb. No offense."

"None taken," she said. He turned away again, and she stripped off her skirt, shirt, bra, her boots and the tattered remains of her tights. She tossed them all in the dumpster. It wasn't like she'd need her Bud's work shirt or the short skirt anymore.

She called for her rabbit and then hopped forward,

ignoring the pain in her leg and nipping at Noah's pant leg. He turned and squatted, grinning at her. "If I try to pet you, you're gonna go all *Monty Python* bunny on me, aren't you?"

She twitched her nose at him, and his grin widened. "Yeah, you are. Here we go, bunny girl."

He picked her up with infinite care and placed her in his backpack before zipping it nearly closed. She braced her body as best she could as Noah eased his bag onto his back. The pack swayed with the movement of his body as he walked toward their building. She heard him open the door and smelled the familiar scent of the lobby as he crossed it to the stairwell. He climbed the two flights of stairs, and she ignored the rib pain when she was jostled around in the backpack.

She heard the stairwell door slam and Noah's soft grunt as he slid the backpack off and set it on the ground. He unzipped it, and she blinked in the light. He lifted her out and put her on the floor in front of her apartment door before placing her purse beside her.

She shifted to her human form, and Noah looked her up and down, muttering a 'damn, girl' before turning to face the other direction. "Why are you sneaking into the building anyway?"

"There's someone I'd rather not talk to waiting for me outside the building," she said.

"Ex-boyfriend?" Noah asked.

"Something like that."

"You need me to talk to him?"

She grinned as she rummaged through her purse for her keys. "Thanks, but no. I'm just grabbing some stuff, and then I'm leaving."

"For good?" He stared at her over his shoulder before turning away again. "Shit, sorry. You leaving for good?"

"Yeah," she said.

"I'm gonna miss you. You've been a good neighbour."

"I'll miss you too," she said, genuinely touched by his words. "Thanks for everything, Noah."

"How are you gonna get back to your car without being seen?" he asked.

"I'll figure something out," she said.

"When you're ready to go, knock on my door. I'll take you back out in the pack," he said.

"I can't ask you to do that," she said.

"You didn't ask. I'm offering. Besides, I'm going out anyway to get me some fuckin' deep dish over at Joe's Pizzeria. I'm starving, and he's open for another hour or so."

She reached out and squeezed his shoulder. "Okay, thanks, Noah."

"Don't mention it." He took the few steps to his door and unlocked it. "See you soon, bunny girl."

CHAPTER 9

Her rabbit was upset. Scratch that. Her rabbit was *pissed*, and she was throwing the mother of all temper tantrums.

Tori gripped the steering wheel hard when her bunny tried to force the shift and take control. "Stop that! Unless you've learned how to drive a fucking car, you taking control right now will just get us both killed."

We can't leave Judd! Please, I don't want to leave him.

"I'm sorry, sweetie, but we have to." Tori took a left. The freeway to the airport was about half a mile away, and her bunny thumped with anger and panic.

He's in danger! We can't leave him unprotected.

"One, he's a bear shifter, and two, he's not in danger. The men who attacked me are dead. Francis won't know that Judd was there or that he helped me," Tori said.

What about the fox shifter?

Dread flashed over her, and she immediately pulled over to the curb, shifting the car into park as she stared at herself in the rear-view mirror. "Shit, the fucking fox shifter."

She took a deep breath, making her ribs ache. "Okay, calm the fuck down. Just because he was staring at you in the bar doesn't mean Francis sent him."

He was outside, too, when the humans showed up. Her bunny reminded her.

She muttered another curse, shoving her hand through her dark hair. "It could just be a coincidence."

If it isn't? What if the fox shifter has told Francis about Judd? He'll try to hurt our mate.

He's not our mate, and we don't know that the fox shifter even works for Francis.

We can't take that risk. Not with our mate.

She sighed and shifted the car into drive, turning it around and heading toward Judd's place. She'd been there once before at a staff barbecue, and although it'd been over a year, she hadn't forgotten where his house was. Not with her obsession with him.

Because he is our mate.

She ignored her bunny but stepped on the gas, anxiety over Judd's safety making her sick to her stomach.

CHRIST, HIS HEAD HURT. JUDD KEPT HIS EYES CLOSED, THE thudding in his temples competing with the steady pulses of pain at the back of his head. Why the fuck did he have such a bad hangover? He rarely drank more than a couple of beers at a time, and besides, it was a fucking work day. He didn't get drunk when he had to go to work.

Linda barked, and he groaned and turned his head back and forth slowly. His bear growled, and the pain in his head rose to an almost unbearable level. He smelled human males, and... what the actual fuck?

He forced his eyes open, blinking rapidly to try to focus. His arms were killing him, and his bear snarled when he tried to move them, and they didn't budge. He stared down at his body. He was sitting on a kitchen chair with his arms tied behind him.

What the hell was going on? He tried to think past the throbbing in his head. He'd gotten home and let Linda out in the backyard to do her business while he replaced his barbells. She'd started barking just as he was finishing up, and he'd gone outside to bring her in. He'd smelled the scent of humans and then...

Clarity washed over him, and he lifted his head to stare at the three humans in his kitchen. His bear growled, and his body swelled. Before he could shift, the closest human snatched up Linda and said, "You shift to your bear, and I'll kill your dog."

His bear retreated immediately. The fucking thing loved Linda as much as Judd's human side did, and his bear made a soft whimper as Judd said, "I'm gonna kill you for touching my dog."

The man laughed. "Jesus, I thought bear shifters were supposed to be tough. First, we get the drop on him in his own backyard. Secondly, he -"

"Because you snuck up behind me like fucking cowards," he snarled. "What the fuck did you hit me with? A two-by-four?"

"A brick, actually," the third man said before striding forward. Judd grunted with pain when he punched him in the stomach. He gasped for air, glaring at the man as the human grinned at the other two. "Not so fucking tough after all."

"I'm gonna rip your fucking throat out," Judd growled.

The man punched him in the face, breaking Judd's nose and rocking his head back to slam against the wall behind him. Fresh pain rocketed through his skull, and he snarled again, baring his teeth at the humans as blood poured out of his nose.

"Uh-uh," the man holding Linda said. "You wanna watch your sweet little puppy die a horrible death? Keep showing us your teeth."

Judd sucked in a breath through his mouth. "What the fuck do you want?"

"*Secondly*, he rolls over and shows us his belly over a fucking dog." The man stared at Linda. "And it's not even a real dog. It's some kind of fucking poodle."

"She's a Pomeranian, you asshole, and she's got bigger fucking balls than you'll ever have," Judd said.

The man rolled his eyes. "Tell me where she hid it, and you and your fucking poodle might live through this."

"Where did who hide what?" Judd asked.

"Tori. Where did she hide it," the man said.

"I have no fucking idea what you're talking about."

"Now, ain't that some bullshit," the man said to the other two humans before turning back to Judd. "You're fucking that rabbit bitch, according to the fox, and women talk in bed. So, where the fuck is it?"

"Go fuck yourself," Judd said.

"Tell me, or I'll kill your dog and then shoot you in the head." The man pointed to the gun tucked into his pants.

Linda barked shrilly and sunk her teeth into the man's hand. He howled and dropped her, kicking at her as she bolted for the kitchen doorway.

"Run, Linda!" Judd shouted. His body swelled, but before he could shift to his bear, the man who'd punched him in the face pressed a gun to his forehead. "Don't, asshole."

"Go get that fucking dog." The leader glared at the second man, holding his bleeding hand.

The man rolled his eyes but left the kitchen. The leader turned to face Judd. "I'm going to wring that dog's neck while you watch, bear shifter."

Linda made a sharp yelp, and Judd's stomach dropped to his fucking feet. Panic rising, he yanked at his bonds as the man dug the gun into his forehead. "Hold the fuck still."

The leader grinned at him as the third man appeared in the doorway. His face was ashen, and he had a hand clamped over his chest. "Boss?"

The leader stared at him. "Where the fuck is the poodle?"

"Boss, I got stabbed. I got…" the man dropped his hand, and Judd stared in disbelief at the hole in his chest. Blood poured from it, and the human dropped to his knees before falling face forward on the kitchen floor.

"What the fuck?" the leader said.

The man holding the gun to Judd's head studied the dead man. "Boss, what's…." Something whistled past Judd's face, and he stared in shock at the knife handle sticking out from the human's chest. The human glanced at Judd before dropping his gun on the floor and touching the knife handle. "What…?"

"No, wait!" The leader shouted as the man yanked on the handle. The knife slid from his chest, and blood spurted out, coating his hands and abdomen as he stared with blank curiosity at the blade before studying the leader.

"I'm bleeding." He toppled over, and his head hit the cupboards with a meaty thud that made Judd's bear growl with satisfaction. He immediately called for his bear, who came forward eagerly but pulled up short when Tori ran into the kitchen, moving impossibly fast.

He watched with dazed shock when she leaped at the last human, climbing him like a fucking tree and wrapping her legs around his hips as she held a silver dagger to his throat. "Hi there."

The man glared at her, his hand reaching for the gun at his waist. "I'm gonna kill you and that fucking poodle, bitch."

"Linda's a Pomeranian, fuckhead." She yanked his head back and slit his throat, hopping off of him and watching with disinterest as the man grabbed his throat and made a gurgling, gasping sound and collapsed. She prodded him in the ribs before wiping off the knife on his shirt and turning to Judd.

"Linda! Where's Linda?" he asked.

The little dog trotted into the kitchen, stopping to sniff at the dead man's leg before sitting in front of Tori. She stared at Tori, panting happily, and Tori patted her head. "You're a good girl, Linda."

She stepped over the dog and reached behind Judd to cut through the ropes that bound him to the chair. He rubbed at his wrists as she studied his face. "You look like shit, Judd."

"Yeah, thanks," he said.

"Hold still," she said. "This will hurt."

She gripped his nose and, with a quick movement, straightened it. Pain lanced through his face, and he grunted out a string of curses before blowing blood out his nose.

"Okay?"

"Just fucking dandy," he growled.

"Pack some stuff. We gotta go," she said.

"Where are we going?" he asked.

"Somewhere safe"

"Tell me what the fuck is going on," he said.

She glanced at the microwave clock. "I will, but we need to leave before he sends more men. He'll send shifters this time."

"Who?" Judd said.

"Francis."

"Who the fuck is Francis?"

Tori bent and picked up Linda before the pooling blood from the dead men could coat her paws. "As soon as we're safe, I'll explain more. Please, Judd. I need you to trust me."

He stared at her before standing. "Give me five minutes."

CHAPTER 10

"Well, it's no Ritz, but it'll do." Tori set her overnight bag on the first double bed as Judd tossed his on the second before setting Linda on the floor. The dog scurried around the motel room, sniffing the loveseat and investigating corners before disappearing into the bathroom.

Tori rubbed at her side. Her thigh was nearly healed, but her ribs still ached like a bitch. She glanced at Judd. "How's your nose?"

"Healed," he said.

She sat down on the bed with a groan. "Christ, I wish I had your healing abilities."

"Your ribs are probably broken," Judd said. "You need to go to the hospital."

"They're not broken," she said.

"Let me guess, you know this because you've had broken ribs before," Judd said.

She nodded. "Did you text Porter that you wouldn't be in for your shift tonight?"

"Yeah. Told him I was sick. You?"

"Same," she said.

Judd ran a hand through his dark hair before grabbing the desk chair and dragging it over to her bed. He sat down and leaned forward, resting his elbows on his thighs. "Start talking, Tori. Who the fuck is trying to kill you?"

"He's not trying to kill me. At least not yet. He needs something from me first," Tori said.

"This Francis guy," Judd said.

"Yeah." Moving carefully, she stuffed some pillows behind her back and leaned against the headboard. "I need to go back further before I met Francis. So, you can understand why I worked for him."

"I'm all fucking ears," Judd said.

Linda returned from the bathroom and stood on her hind legs, resting her front paws against the bed and staring earnestly at Tori. Judd lifted the little dog and set her on the bed.

Linda circled on the bed several times before lying down and resting her chin on Tori's shin. She heaved a heavy sigh and closed her eyes. Tori petted her soft head. "She's a cute dog. How long have you had her?"

"Since she was a year old. She's eight now," Judd said.

Tori glanced at him. "You love her a lot."

"Yes," he said without any embarrassment.

She stroked Linda's soft ears as Judd made an impatient sound. "Tori…"

She took a deep breath. "My mother was a rabbit shifter, and my father was a wolverine shifter."

"Holy fuck," Judd said. "I know prey and predators sometimes mate, but it's usually a larger prey animal, like a zebra or a deer."

"They were an odd couple, and their families were… concerned, to say the least. But they made it work. They loved each other a great deal."

86

"I guess this explains why you're so fucking tough," Judd said. "You've got a wolverine personality in a bunny body."

She laughed. "I drove my mom crazy as a kid. I was fearless and had no real sense of danger. I was born a year after my parents were married. When I was two, my father was murdered in an armed robbery. He was at a convenience store at the wrong time. Took two bullets to the head and died instantly."

"I'm sorry," Judd said.

She studied Linda's soft brown fur. "My mother is… she's a good person, but she doesn't have a lot of common sense, nor does she have a good sense for people. She's naive and too trusting, like most bunnies, and she was… lonely."

"She remarried quickly?" Judd asked.

"No, she'd loved my father a great deal and often told me he was the only one for her. Which was true in a certain sense, but deciding she'd never marry again didn't stop the loneliness or her libido. As I was growing up, there were many men in and out of our lives."

Judd stiffened. "Did they hurt you?"

"Oh God, no," Tori said. "They were all prey animals like my mother, mostly bunnies, and they were perfectly nice guys. Hell, some of them even stuck around for a few years, but my mother's inability to move on, and her obvious love for my dead father, didn't exactly scream healthy relationship between her and whatever guy she was currently banging. It also didn't stop her from having kit after kit."

"Rabbits like to have babies," Judd said. "Everyone knows that."

"I have nineteen half-siblings," Tori said.

Judd's jaw dropped. "You're fucking with me."

"I'm not," Tori said. "There was an emptiness in my mother that she tried to fill with kits."

She stroked Linda's fur again, smiling when the little dog rolled to her side so Tori could pet her belly. "She basically raised all of us as a single mom. Sure, there were men here and there, but, as I said, they never stayed for more than a few years. She had nineteen kids with fourteen different men, and while most of them paid child support, it was still difficult growing up. We never had enough of anything. Food, money, space, or privacy. I shared a room with five sisters until I moved out at eighteen."

She rubbed lightly at her ribs. "In university, I decided to get my bachelor's degree in environmental sciences for sustainability. I was obsessed with what overpopulation is doing to our planet and its ability to sustain life."

"You don't actually have children, do you?" Judd said.

She shook her head. "Nope. The pictures I showed you were of my nieces and nephew."

"So, you don't want cubs?" Judd's voice was neutral, but she could see and smell his disappointment.

Was he disappointed because he wanted children with her? Her stomach made a weird clench, and her bunny's happiness skyrocketed.

"No, I want kits," Tori said. "But only a couple."

Judd sat back in his chair, and she could practically smell the relief pouring off him. Ignoring her bunny's excitement that Judd wanted children, too, she said, "Shortly before I graduated, I went to a climate change and overpopulation discussion at the university. The keynote speaker was an antelope shifter and scientist named Francis. He was passionate about climate change and how overpopulation was affecting our planet. I was in awe of him. I sat in the audience, and for the first time in my life, I felt like someone else finally understood me. After the conference, I introduced myself to him, and we ended up going for coffee. We talked for hours, Judd.

Everything Francis said and thought was a mirror of how I felt."

She stared at the ceiling, studying the chips and dents that marred the white paint. "Francis offered me a job working with him as soon as I graduated."

"Doing what?" Judd asked.

"At first, research into climate change and overpopulation." She closed her eyes, but her exhaustion wasn't what made her memories fuzzy.

"What do you mean at first?" Judd said.

"Francis was making a name for himself in certain environmental circles. He did many rallies and speeches about climate change and how it was killing the planet. He made a lot of enemies."

"Were you in danger?" Judd asked.

"I didn't think so, but Francis…" she took a deep breath, "he'd become like a substitute father to me by that point. He wasn't married and had no kids, but he treated me like his daughter. Anyway, I traveled with him to most of his conferences, I'd been photographed with him a lot, and he was worried for my safety. He encouraged me to take self-defense courses and even paid for them."

"That's good," Judd said.

"Turns out I was good at that kind of shit. Self-defense courses turned into martial art classes, weapons training, and hand-to-hand combat." She smiled at Judd. "I liked it, probably a little too much, and I liked how surprised others were when I could kick their ass."

He grinned. "Yeah, there aren't many bunny assassins in the world."

She rolled her eyes. "Enough with the assassin shit, big guy."

"So, you were still doing research for this Francis guy?" Judd prompted.

"Yes, until one night we were out for dinner after this big rally he'd spoken at about climate change. There were protesters at the rally, which wasn't unusual. We always had protesters anytime Francis spoke about climate change. It's," she made a face, "a very decisive topic."

"Isn't that the fucking truth," Judd said.

"Anyway, it was just him and me, and it was a normal night, you know? We usually went out for dinner after a speech. It was kind of a ritual for us."

"What happened?" Judd asked.

"We were walking back to the car, and this guy came out of nowhere. He was one of the protesters, and he had a gun. He was certifiably loony-tunes. The police said later that he'd been arrested multiple times for bringing weapons to rallies, for threatening speakers, that sort of thing. Anyway, he tried to kill Francis, and I stopped him."

Judd stared at her. "You stopped him."

"Yes. I disarmed him in about twenty seconds flat. It was easy. I barely broke a sweat, but Francis was shocked at how good I was at it. And he knew me, you know?" She gave Judd a sick look. "He could see how much I fucking liked it. Could see that it got me amped up, and so he made me the head of his security."

"Security," Judd said. "You didn't do research for him anymore?"

"No," Tori said. "The threats on his life had gradually been ramping up, and he was worried that more people would attack him. Honestly, he was right to be worried. He was making a lot of enemies with his refusal to sugarcoat how badly we were fucking the planet and how strongly he believed that overpopulation was the biggest contributor."

"So, you became his bodyguard, and then what?" Judd asked. "Why did you leave? Why is he after you? The men at my house wanted to know where you hid it. What did they mean by that?"

"I don't know," she said, rubbing her forehead.

"They seemed pretty confident that you took something that belonged to this Francis guy," Judd said. "You're telling me you didn't?"

"I'm telling you, I don't know," she said flatly. She glanced at the bedside clock. It was just after seven in the morning, and she didn't have time to sleep despite her weariness. Unless Judd was agreeable to fleeing the country with her.

"Hey, you wouldn't be agreeable to fleeing the country with me, would you?" she asked.

He stared at her. "What?"

"Leaving everything and everyone you know and spending the rest of your life in hiding. Does that sound like something you might be interested in?"

"No," he said.

She sighed. "Yeah, I didn't think so."

She slid off the bed, grateful that her ribs hurt less. "Okay, give me fifteen minutes to shower bad guy blood off of me, and then we'll go."

"Go where?" Judd asked.

"To see a witch."

CHAPTER 11

Judd stepped out of the elevator and followed Tori down the apartment building hallway.

"How do you know a witch lives here?" he asked when she knocked briskly on one of the doors.

"You hear things in my line of work," she said.

"Your line of work as an assassin or a server?" he asked.

She wrinkled her nose at him, and despite how worried and tired he was, he couldn't help but grin. Teasing Tori came as naturally as breathing to him.

The door opened, and Judd's bear chuffed in surprise. A slender brunette with pretty blue eyes stood in the doorway. The largest crow Judd had ever seen sat on her shoulder.

"Can I help you?" the brunette said.

"Are you Helen?" Tori asked.

"No, that's my grandmother."

"I need to speak with her."

"She's not here," the brunette said.

"When will she return?"

The woman grinned. "In the spring. She's visiting her sister in the old country for the winter."

"Fuck." Tori studied the woman. "Are you a witch like your grandmother?"

"I am," she said.

"You'll have to do." Tori sighed and pushed her way past the woman and into the apartment.

The woman stared at Judd, who said, "Uh, sorry, we have a bit of a situation happening."

"Right. Well, come on in," she said.

Judd followed her inside, and she led him and Tori down a narrow hallway to the living room. A mid-sized wooden altar was pushed against the far wall, and a tall and curvy blonde woman stood next to it. The air smelled like incense and herbs, and candles flickered on every flat surface in the room.

The blonde woman used a mortar and pestle to grind something at the altar. As they watched, she stopped and studied an open book beside her on the altar. "Oh my God, Elora. I must have done something wrong. The book says it should be a light green colour and paste-like, and mine looks like liquid brown vomit. What have I -"

She stopped as she glanced up and saw Tori and Judd. "Um, who are your friends?"

"No idea," Elora said cheerfully. "They're looking for Helen."

"I'm looking for a witch," Tori said. "A powerful one."

She glanced at the blonde woman who said, "Don't look at me. I'm a witch by apprenticeship, and honestly, not a very good one."

"Don't sell yourself short, Cece," Elora said. "You've only been a witch for six months. It takes time to learn."

Elora petted the sleek feathers of the crow still sitting on her shoulder. "Cece has definite potential. Even Helen says so, and she's usually a real jerk to apprentice witches. I'm Elora, by the way."

"I'm Tori, and this is Judd." Tori studied the altar and the candles.

"Man, you're a big guy." Elora looked him up and down. "You're a shifter, I assume?"

Judd nodded. "Black bear."

"Cool."

"It's nice to meet you." Judd held out his hand to Elora, yanking it back when the crow snapped its beak and stared at him with murder in its black eyes.

"Sorry, Lilianna doesn't care much for men," Elora said. "She gets all snappy-snappy with her beak if they get too close."

Judd sniffed at the bird. "That isn't just a crow."

"Tell me about it," Elora said as Lilianna flew off her shoulder to a high perch close to the altar. "So, what do you need a witch for?"

"I need a memory spell," Tori said.

"Do you want to remember or forget?" Elora asked.

"Remember. I had an amnesia spell cast on me, and now I need it removed."

Judd stared at Tori, shock rippling over him as Elora said, "They're hard to break."

"I know," Tori said. "Which is why I wanted your grandmother. She's the most powerful witch in the city."

Cece left her spot by the altar to join them. "Elora is powerful too."

"Then she should have no problems breaking the spell." Tori shrugged out of her leather jacket and laid it across the couch.

"How long have you been under the spell?" Elora asked.

"Not exactly certain of the time frame, but at least a few years," Tori said.

Elora frowned. "Why do you want to break it now?"

Tori stared at Judd. "Because I'm tired of running."

"TORI, ARE YOU SURE THIS IS A GOOD IDEA?" JUDD STOOD next to Tori, watching Elora and Cece look through a colossal-sized book that Elora had pulled off the bookshelf. "She looks about sixteen years old. What's a teenager know about breaking a spell?"

"I'm twenty-four," Elora looked over at him, her blue eyes narrowed with anger, "and maybe try being a little more respectful, or I'll do a binding spell that permanently seals your mouth shut."

His bear growled in alarm, and Judd took an involuntary step back. Elora stared him down for a few more seconds before giggling. "I'm totally kidding. I would never do magic with the intent of harming someone."

Judd glared at her, and Elora laughed again. "Look, I know I'm young, but - and no offense - you two seem kind of desperate and not like you have time to find a more powerful witch. Am I right?"

"You're right." Tori elbowed Judd lightly in the stomach. "He'll be quiet."

"What if the spell doesn't work?" Judd lowered his voice. "What if she makes you forget even more shit instead of remembering? What if you don't remember -"

He shut his mouth abruptly. Tori didn't need to know how pathetic it made him that he was terrified she wouldn't remember him.

Tori reached up and cupped his face. "Judd, I won't forget you. Ever."

He studied her mouth, his urge to kiss her too overwhelming to ignore. He pressed his lips against hers. "You don't know that for sure."

"I do," she breathed against his lips. "I won't forget you, no matter what."

He kissed her again, but she pulled back and looked at the witches when he tried to deepen it. Elora had joined them, a large grin on her pretty face. "You two are so sweet together. How long have you been a couple?"

"We're not," Tori said, stepping back from Judd. "Can you break the spell or not?"

"We're about to find out," Elora said. "But before I do, there is the matter of payment. It's five hundred to break the spell. I accept cash, Venmo, or Paypal."

"Five hundred?" Judd said. "That's a lot of fucking money."

"It's a lot of fucking spell," Elora said. "Plus, breaking an amnesia spell isn't exactly allowed by the WWC without their written permission. So, that means danger pay for me."

Judd snorted. "Danger pay. The WWC will fine you, nothing more."

"Maybe, maybe not," Elora said. "The council has been cracking down on the dark magic as of late."

"Wait, this is dark magic?" Cece gave Elora an alarmed look.

"Technically, no," Elora said. "An amnesia spell is considered dark magic, just because so many people use it for the wrong reasons, but breaking it isn't considered dark magic. Mostly."

"Mostly? What does mostly mean?" Cece asked.

Tori grabbed her jacket and pulled a flat leather pouch

from the inside pocket. Judd watched in surprise as she peeled off five one hundred dollar bills from a large wad of cash and handed it to Elora.

"Thank you," Elora said.

"We're getting that back if this doesn't work," Judd said.

"Of course. I have a rock solid spell satisfaction guarantee," Elora said. "If it doesn't work, I'll even throw the next spell in for free."

"Why would we want a free spell from a witch who couldn't make the first spell work?" Judd asked.

"Oh, you are a cheeky bear," Elora said. "I like you. If you weren't so obviously smitten with Tori, I'd ask you out on a date."

Lilianna cawed loudly from her perch before flying across the room to land on Elora's shoulder. She stared unblinkingly at Judd, her beak opening and shutting slowly on repeat.

"Jesus, that crow is fucking creepy," Judd said.

"She isn't." Elora petted Lilianna, who leaned in so she could groom Elora's hair with her beak without taking her gaze from Judd. "She's just very protective of me and suspicious of men. Which is nice, but also, between you and me, she's one hell of a cock blocker."

Cece laughed, and even Tori grinned as Elora rubbed her hands together and said, "Who's ready to do some magic?"

Ten minutes later, Judd and his bear watched with apprehension as Elora, now wearing a dark robe, had Tori kneel on a cushion before the altar. Cece, also wearing a dark robe, extinguished the candles in the living room one by one.

Before we start, are you paranormal or human?" Elora asked.

"Rabbit shifter, why?" Tori said.

"I use different candles for paranormals," Elora said. A large antique wooden cabinet stood next to the altar, and

Elora opened it before rummaging through the shelves. Cece joined her, and although she spoke in a whisper, Judd had no problem hearing her.

"Elora, are you sure about this? The fire spells are the hardest to control," Cece said.

"I know," Elora said. "It'll be fine. I'm an elemental witch, for God's sake. Fire is my specialty."

"It will be eventually," Cece said, "but your grandmother specifically told you not to do any fire spells while she was gone. Remember the last time you did a fire spell?"

"What happened the last time you did a fire spell?" Judd said loudly.

Elora gathered three dark blue pillar candles and one red tapered candle from the cabinet, glancing at him over her shoulder. "One small teensy-weensy flame maybe, kind of, got out of control. It was nothing to worry about."

Judd studied the scorch marks on the ceiling. "Your ceiling suggests there was something to worry about."

Elora just shrugged as she set the candles on the altar and lit the red one. "Look, a fire spell is the only way to restore her memories."

"You sure? Maybe we should stick with something safer like a water spell," Judd said.

"I can't drown the memory back into her," Elora said. "Flame illuminates and reveals. It has to be a fire spell."

"It'll be fine," Tori said. "Start the spell, Elora."

Judd's bear made an uneasy whine as Elora picked up the red candle. She stood in front of Tori. "This will hurt, but it can't be helped."

"Just do it," Tori said.

"Tilt your head back," Elora said.

Tori tilted her head back, and Elora dripped wax from the burning candle onto her forehead. Judd's bear growled when

Tori hissed out a breath, and Cece, standing next to the altar, gave him a nervous look.

Elora lit the dark blue candles before studying the heavy book on the altar. The back of Judd's neck prickled, and his bear whimpered quietly when Elora read from the book. She spoke what sounded like complete gibberish to Judd, and he clenched his hands into fists, ignoring his urge to simply pick up Tori and run out of the apartment with her.

Elora's voice rose and fell as she chanted the incantation. The flames on the candles grew larger and brighter, and Lilianna cawed loudly from her perch, flapping her long wings before settling down.

Elora picked up one of the candles and held it in her hand as she stared into the flame.

"By my power, flame and fire, restore what once was lost."

The flame flared brighter, and Elora reached out to touch Tori's forehead, resting the palm of her free hand against the wax that clung to it.

"By my power, flame and fire, restore what once was lost. By my power, flame and fire, restore what once was lost. By my power, flame and fire, restore what once was lost."

Tori made a low cry of pain, and Judd's bear surged forward. He held his bear back with iron willpower and squinted at the altar as the flames from the three candles grew impossibly bright.

Her face pale and her voice strained, Elora shouted, "By my power, flame and fire, restore what once was lost!"

There was a loud popping sound, and Elora and Cece cried out when the flames shot out from all three candles so high they licked at the ceiling. Tori made a hoarse cry of pain as Elora dropped the candle and staggered back before falling to her knees.

Judd ran forward, pushing past the fallen witch and scooping up Tori. Her head fell back, and he could see the whites of her eyes as her body shook wildly. His bear roared with fear, and he turned toward Elora as CeCe used a blanket to extinguish the flames flickering to life on Tori's cushion.

"What did you do?" he snarled as Elora climbed to her feet.

He set Tori on the couch and stepped toward Elora, his bear growling loudly. He ducked when Lilianna flew at him, cawing and pecking viciously at him with her beak. He roared in pain when she gouged out a piece of flesh just above his eyebrow.

"Fucking crow!" he snarled, baring his teeth at her when Lilianna dive-bombed him again.

He sidestepped, barely avoiding Lilianna's beak from plucking out his eyeball.

"Lilianna, stop!" Elora shouted.

Still cawing, Lilianna flew to Elora, settling on her shoulder and grooming her hair repeatedly as Elora held her hand in a stay-back gesture at Judd. "Tori's okay. She's just… she's okay, I promise."

"She's having a seizure!" he snapped before hurrying toward Tori. Her body had stopped shaking, but she was pale and limp. He eased her into a sitting position, cradling her against him as he stroked her cheek. "Tori, baby, wake up. Wake up, Tori-girl."

Her eyelids fluttered, and he breathed a sigh of relief when she opened her eyes and stared at him.

"There you are, Tori-girl," he said. "You scared me."

She blinked at him a few times before touching his face. "Who are you?"

Judd's stomach crashed to the fucking apartment below

them. Before he could say anything, Tori grinned at him. "Just kidding, big guy."

"Jesus Christ," he said, "don't you ever fucking do that to me again."

She laughed and leaned against his chest, peeling off the wax that clung to her forehead with a grimace. "I feel like I've been hit by a truck. My head is killing me."

"Did it work?" Elora asked. "Do you remember?"

Judd's body tensed as he stared down at Tori. She took his hand, linking their fingers as she stared at the witch. "I remember."

CHAPTER 12

"Thank you." Tori accepted the cup of tea from Elora and took a sip.

It was delicious, hot and steamy with a hint of peppermint, and her bunny thumped happily as she drank another swallow.

The china teacup looking ridiculous in his big hand, Judd gave her a worried look. "How's your head?"

"A little better." She touched the almost healed gouge that was above his eyebrow. "What happened here?"

"Fucking crow is what happened," Judd said with a murderous look at Lilianna.

She stared coolly back at him before grooming her feathers. Elora sat in the chair across from the couch. She looked tired but elated and smiled at Cece in the chair beside her. "I did it, Cece. I did it!"

"And only set one cushion on fire," Judd said.

Elora laughed. "I know you're mocking me, but seriously, we're super lucky I didn't burn down the whole apartment. That was a ridiculously complicated spell."

Judd rolled his eyes before setting the teacup on the

coffee table and standing. "Well, this has been great, but we gotta go. Come on, Tori."

He held out his hand, staring at her when she didn't move. "What?"

"I need another spell broken," she said.

"Are you fucking kidding me? She almost set the apartment on fire with the last one."

"One tiny cushion caught on fire," Elora protested.

Tori took his hand, tugging him back onto the couch beside her. "We need her, Judd."

He sighed and sat back as Elora said, "What kind of spell this time?"

"A protection spell."

"Against a person or an object?" Elora asked.

"An object," Tori said.

"There are thousands of different protection spells. I'll need a little more than that from you."

"I can remember part of the incantation the warlock was using to break the protection spell," Tori said.

"How powerful is this warlock? Did he create the protection spell as well?" Elora asked.

"Yes," Tori said. "I think he was fairly powerful. He was a scientist who worked with Francis, and Francis only hires the best."

"Francis?" Cece asked.

"Francis Schmelzle," Tori said as if that explained everything.

"Is Francis a good guy or a bad guy?" Elora asked.

"A name with that many consonants can only point to evil intent," Cece said.

"Francis is the fucking worst," Tori said. "He wears cowboy boots he didn't earn and is the least trustworthy person ever."

"Good call," Elora said to Cece. "Where is the warlock now? Does he still work for this Francis guy? If so, maybe I could talk to him - witch to warlock - and get him to release the protection spell."

"He's dead," Tori said.

"Plan B, then," Elora said. "I need you to write down what you remember of the incantation, and then I'll need to do some research. Leave me your numbers, and I'll text when I know which one it is."

"How much?" Tori asked as she set her teacup on the coffee table and stood.

"I won't know until, or *if*, I can figure out what kind of protection spell it is," Elora said. "But it's gonna be at least another five hundred."

Judd snorted, and Elora grinned at him. "I promise not to set anything on fire this time."

"Can you even make that kind of promise?" Judd asked.

"No," Elora said sadly. "I set a lot of things on fire."

Tori and Cece laughed, and even though he was trying to hide it, Tori knew Judd liked the little witch.

As Judd stood, Tori smiled at Elora. "Get me some paper, and I'll write down what I remember."

———

"I took Linda outside to do her business and I picked up some food while you were showering." Tori pointed to the fast food bags sitting on the desk.

"Thanks," Judd said. "I'm starving."

She didn't doubt it. It was close to noon, and if Judd was like most bear shifters, he rarely missed a meal.

He walked over to his bed and rummaged through his overnight bag. He wore just a pair of shorts, and his thick dark hair was damp. He rubbed a towel over it absentmind-edly as he pulled out a t-shirt. Tori studied his perfect naked chest and tried not to drool.

Her bunny was going mad, begging and pleading for Tori to fuck him, and it was getting harder and harder to ignore her. Especially now that she knew how it felt to be fucked by Judd.

Judd glanced her way, sniffing the air, and hot embarrass-ment flooded her. She immediately went into the bathroom, closing the door and leaning against it. It was warm and steamy from Judd's shower, and she stared at herself in the foggy mirror. So, Judd could smell her lust for him. So, what? That was nothing new.

No, but being alone in a motel room with him is some-thing new. Fucking him last night was something new.

She sighed and used the bathroom before washing her hands and, telling her bunny to calm the fuck down already, opened the bathroom door. Judd sat on his bed with the food and Linda, who stared eagerly at him. He'd pulled on a t-shirt, thank Christ, but even the sight of his bare legs covered in dark hair was enough to get her motor running. Apprehen-sion, lust, and nerves rolling around in her belly, she joined him, sitting cross-legged beside him as he handed her a burger and a carton of fries.

"Thank you," she said.

"You're welcome." He ate a few fries from his carton, grinning when Linda put her front paws on one thick thigh and stared at the fries. He pointed to her empty food dish on the floor next to the bag of dog food. "You already had your lunch, sweetpea."

Tori unwrapped her burger and bit into it. It was nothing special, but she hadn't eaten since last night's dinner break and figured she was nearly as hungry as Judd. She stuffed another bite into her mouth, chewing it down before laughing when Judd gave Linda a fry.

"I thought she already had her lunch."

Judd grinned a little sheepishly. "My sweetpea loves French fries. Don't you, pretty girl?"

Linda barked excitedly, and Judd shook his head. "No barking, Linda. Sit."

The little dog sat on the bed, her body excitedly vibrating as Judd tore off a piece of his burger and fed it to her.

"Okay, enough treats. Go lie down, sweetpea."

Tori watched in amazement as Linda wandered to the end of the bed and circled three times before curling up into a ball. She rested her chin on her paws and stared at Judd as he ate the rest of his burger in five large bites.

"She's a good dog," Tori said.

"She's the best dog," Judd corrected.

"Did you have dogs growing up?" Tori asked.

"Nah, my mom was allergic. I wasn't even planning on getting a dog, but I was at the city rescue with a friend who wanted a dog, and I saw Linda. It was love at first sight," he said.

"Why was she at the rescue?"

"Her family had a baby and decided Linda was too much work."

"People suck," Tori said.

"Yeah." He ate the rest of his fries and drank half his soda as she finished her burger. He eyed her half-eaten carton of fries, and she handed them to him.

"You don't want them?" he asked.

She shook her head. "I'm full."

He ate the fries, tossing one more to Linda before gathering the garbage and stuffing it into the bin near the desk. He returned to the bed, stretching out his long legs and leaning back against the headboard.

She studied his body, her lust roaring back to life, and Judd groaned softly. "Tori-girl, you're killing me over here."

"Sorry." She looked away, studying the wallpaper as Judd cleared his throat. She couldn't sleep with Judd again, despite what her bunny wanted.

"Tell me why Francis is after you," Judd said.

She grabbed a pillow and hugged it to herself. "It's a long story. Maybe we should get some sleep first. We're both exhausted."

He shook his head. "I won't be able to sleep until I know what the fuck is going on."

She sighed and leaned back against the headboard. "Six years ago, Francis lost his fucking mind...."

CHAPTER 13

Six Years Ago

"Morning, Tori."

She glanced up from her laptop, studying the dark-haired zebra shifter standing in the doorway. "Hey, Rick. How was your weekend?"

"Gaming tournament. I kicked ass."

She laughed. "Nice. Did you get my email about prepping for the conference? The protesters are already showing up at the hotel. We'll need to take Francis in through the back a day earlier than planned."

"I read it this morning." Rick crossed his arms over his chest and leaned against the doorway. "It's getting worse. Every time he speaks now, there are protesters and death threats."

"I know," she said, "but Francis speaks a lot of truths that people don't want to hear."

"Climate change seems to bring out the crazies on both sides," Rick said.

"You calling me crazy?" Francis clapped Rick on the shoulder before squeezing past him.

"No, Boss." Rick had the good grace to look embarrassed. "How was your weekend?"

"Fine." Francis studied him for a few seconds before giving a dismissive wave. "Leave. I need to speak with Astoria."

Rick grimaced and stepped back as Francis shut the door in his face. Francis turned, shrugging at the look Tori gave him. "What?"

"You were rude to Rick."

He walked across her small office, sinking into the chair across from her desk. "He's a nobody. I don't fucking care about Rick."

"You should. He's one of the security guys responsible for keeping you safe."

Francis crossed his leg, resting his ankle against his knee and running his fingers over the stitching on his cowboy boots. Tori hated those fucking boots.

"A zebra shifter as security is a fucking joke anyway," Francis said.

"Says the man with a bunny shifter leading his security team."

"You're different. You're special," Francis said.

"You missed dinner on Saturday," Tori said.

He stared blankly at her, and she said, "We were having dinner together at the diner."

"No, you were having dinner with Tamatha and Dan at their farm," Francis said.

"That was last Saturday," she said.

His phone dinged, and he pulled it from his pocket to scan

the screen. "I thought you went to their house every Saturday night because of how old they are. Hell, I'm surprised they haven't dropped dead already."

She stared at him, keeping her mouth shut with Herculean effort. Francis knew how important Tamatha and Dan were to her, and for him to be so cavalier regarding them spoke volumes about her deteriorating relationship with him.

He ran a hand through his hair before staring at his phone screen again. "Yeah, okay, I forgot about our dinner."

The hurt threatened to swallow her whole. Her relationship with Francis used to be the most important one in her life but over the last two years…

He's changed. He's changed in ways that are confusing and frightening. He isn't the same guy he used to be.

She wanted to ignore her inner voice, wanted to pretend that Francis was just different because he was tired or busy or wrapped up in his all-consuming desire to make the world see how badly they were fucking their planet.

Only, she couldn't. Not anymore, anyway. Over the last year or so, he'd started behaving differently. Treating those who worked for him like they didn't matter, spending too many late nights and weekends here at the office or in his lab. He was working on something in the lab, something he'd hired a whole fucking team of scientists to do, but he refused to tell her what it was.

He used to share everything with her, but now there was a distance between them that, despite her best efforts, she couldn't breach. Who Francis was had fundamentally changed, and it was impossible to ignore.

Or maybe this is who he's been all along, and your need for a father blinded you.

Hurt turned to simmering anxiety. She prided herself on seeing people for who they were, and she didn't know what was worse - her dying relationship with Francis or the idea that she had been entirely wrong about him for all these years.

Either way, now wasn't the time to delve into her personal feelings. She had a fucking job to do.

"There's talk about the protesters doing a little more than protesting at the conference," Tori said.

Francis didn't look up from his phone. "There's always talk of that."

"It's different this time," Tori said. "I think you should cancel the conference."

That got his attention.

He tucked his phone into his pocket and folded his hands across his flat abdomen before sniffing in her direction. "You're actually nervous about this one, aren't you."

"Yes," she said. "They're out to kill you, Francis."

"Hire more security," he said.

She leaned forward, trying to keep her patience. "That isn't the answer. Do you know how many death threats you've had over the last week?"

"Two hundred and seven," he said.

"That's right. Four different people have tried to break into your home in the last month, Francis. I know you want to save the planet, and I get that, but it's not worth your life."

"It is!" he snapped. Brown fur grew on his face, and the tips of his sharp antlers poked out from his skull. "This planet will be fucked by the next generation, Astoria. I will not stand by and do nothing just because a few assholes don't want to hear the truth."

"It's not working," she said softly. "The rallies, the conferences, trying to educate them… it's not enough. You're risking your life for something that isn't making a difference."

She waited for his rage. Antelope shifters were usually timid by nature, but, like her, Francis was an exception to his kind. His anger always lurked at the surface, barely hidden behind a mask of politeness.

"You're right," he said. "The conferences, the speeches, they aren't doing fuck all to change the Neanderthals' way of thinking. They're perfectly content to keep fucking each other, content to keep bringing new life into a planet that can barely sustain human life as it is."

Surprise washed over her at his admittance.

"Then why are you still doing them?" she asked. "Why are you risking your life for something you know doesn't work?"

He shrugged. "It's expected of me. It keeps the investors off my back while I…."

"While you what? Work on whatever it is you're cooking up in the lab?"

"What do you know about that?" he asked.

"Nothing, because you won't tell me anything. You used to tell me everything, Francis. There were no secrets between us. Remember?"

He studied her for long silent moments. "I wanted to tell you, but you weren't ready."

"Ready for what?"

"To understand the truth," he said. "But I think you finally see it now."

"Francis, you're talking in fucking riddles," she said.

He grinned and stood up. "C'mon, let's go to the lab."

Five minutes later, they stood in the wide hallway outside the lab. Francis punched in the keycode, and the doors slid open. She followed him into a peaceful world of white walls and hushed voices. They passed a few different rooms, the shifters in them barely looking up from their lab equipment as they walked by. A room full of rabbits in cages made her pause.

"None of them are shifters." Francis stood beside her as she stared at the cages.

"That doesn't make it better," she said. "You're still experimenting on them."

"We aren't harming or killing them," he said. "Nancy in biotech has already taken three of them home as pets."

She just stared at him, and Francis shrugged. "It's for the greater good. Besides, we don't need them anymore, anyway."

"What do you mean?"

"You'll see. C'mon, we're almost there."

She followed him into the central lab. A bank of floor-to-ceiling glass door coolers made a low hum on the far wall. Racks of purple liquid in small vials filled nearly one cooler.

She stared at the human standing in the middle of the room. His white lab coat had purple stains across the chest and the sleeve edges, and he was short with thinning hair and round wire-rimmed glasses that reminded Tori of the ones John Lennon used to wear. He stood in front of a massive steel table with various lab equipment and a gray metal box roughly eighteen by eighteen inches in size. The box was smooth and unblemished by seams. The right side held a thin panel with three black buttons.

As Tori and Francis watched, the man pressed the first button. With a whirring, clicking sound, the middle of the box opened, and a silver tube rose out of the opening.

The human pushed the second button, and a delicate purple mist emitted from the tube, rising lazily into the air before dissipating. Francis giggled and clapped his hands as the man pushed the final button, the tube slid back into the box, and the lid closed.

"It's working," Francis said.

The man nodded. "Yes, although I need to tweak the mechanism to give us a larger delivery radius."

"Plenty of time for that," Francis said. "You're well ahead of schedule."

"Human trials aren't fully completed yet," the man said.

"I'm aware," Francis said irritably.

He joined the man at the table, and after a moment, Tori followed him.

"Astoria, this is Edgar Steinwell, the lead scientist on Project Purple. Edgar, this is Astoria Baker, head of my security."

Astoria shook the man's hand. "Nice to meet you."

"You as well."

"What's Project Purple?" Astoria asked.

Francis rubbed his hands together. "It's the solution to our problem."

"What do you mean?"

"Overpopulation is killing our planet, but humans refuse to listen. They keep breeding like rabbits - no offense - and refuse to accept the consequences. They've left me no choice, Astoria. This is for their own good."

She studied him, her stomach clenching and her rabbit making soft thumps. "What have you done, Francis?"

He smiled dreamily at the vials of purple liquid in the cooler. "I've created a serum, or rather, Edgar has created a serum that sterilizes humans and paranormals."

Disbelief washed over her. "You can't be serious."

He frowned at her. "I am. We're going to use the liquid and," he pointed at the box, "this device to sterilize the entire city."

"You can't sterilize the humans and the paranormals against their consent," Tori said.

"They've left me no choice," he repeated.

She stared at the box, and her rabbit thumped again as she stepped back from the table. "The purple mist, it..."

"The serum is ingested by breathing in the mist. We've engineered it to stay in the atmosphere for over forty-eight hours, but Edgar assures me that it will also easily seep into buildings and vehicles through the smallest openings," Francis said.

Her hand went to her stomach as her bunny thumped with panic. "Did you just fucking sterilize me, Francis?"

He shook his head. "Of course not, Astoria, don't be ridiculous. The serum only works on those with XY chromosomes, and the mist you just saw is water with a bit of purple food colouring."

She grabbed the table to steady herself as Francis, oblivious to her distress, gave her a gleeful grin. "We started clinical trials on the paranormals and humans six months ago."

"Francis, if you sterilize everyone, paranormals and humans will -"

"We're not sterilizing everyone," Francis said. "One of our biggest obstacles in creating the serum was sterilizing only some and not all of the population. Happily, our initial trials show the humans and paranormals are solving the problem themselves."

"What do you mean?"

"Two percent of humans with XY chromosomes have a genetic mutation that prevents sterilization from the serum. Forty-seven percent of paranormals with XY chromosomes have the same genetic mutation. So, you see, problem solved," Francis said.

"This is what you've been working on here in the lab for the last two years," Tori said, before looking at Edgar.

"Yes. Well, Edgar just joined the project last year. Before

him, we were getting nowhere with it, but then…" Francis made a fluttering motion with his hands. "Magic."

When Tori stared blankly at him, he laughed. "Literally magic."

She turned to study Edgar again. "You're a warlock."

"Yes," Edgar said.

"We were lucky to find him," Francis said. "There are not many scientific-minded individuals who happen to be warlocks, as well. Within six months, he had a working version of the serum on animals. Three months later, he'd altered it to work on humans and paranormals. He's fucking brilliant. Isn't that right, Edgar?"

Edgar nodded but didn't say anything. Tori was surprised by his modesty. Of course, maybe this was normal behaviour for him. She didn't know the fucking guy… beyond that, he was about to be responsible for the mass sterilization of nearly an entire city.

"Francis, sterilizing the city isn't -"

"Not just the city," Francis said. "We'll start here, but even if we sterilized every male human and paranormal in the city, it wouldn't be nearly enough. You know that. But if we expand it…."

"Expand it," Tori repeated. He couldn't mean what she thought. Not even Francis would be that radical.

Sterilizing an entire fucking city isn't radical enough for you?

"Across the world," Francis said. "With only two percent of humans and roughly fifty percent of paranormals able to procreate, our overpopulation problem is solved. Climate change will slow, potentially even be reversed. Our world will survive, Astoria."

"Francis, what you're saying is… it's crazy."

His eyes narrowed, and that familiar stubborn look

crossed his face. "What's crazy is watching our planet die when I can do something to save it. You admitted yourself that what we're doing isn't working. This will work. While I will admit that mass sterilization is on the extreme end, what choice do we have?"

"You can choose not to take people's choice away from them," she said. "This isn't the way, Francis."

"It's the only way, Astoria." Francis's voice turned cold like a winter wind. "And you are either with me or against me."

Sorrow washed over her in a heavy rush, making her feel like her very bones were cracking in half. The man she'd considered a father was gone. He'd been replaced by an insane zealot who wouldn't hesitate to destroy anyone who stood in his path... including her.

She stared directly at him, the cold survival instinct swallowing her sorrow. "I'm with you, Francis."

"Are you?" he asked.

She didn't look away from him, didn't let the fear and the hurt bubbling deep in her guts take a single step toward the light. "I'm *always* with you."

He smiled and stepped toward her, cupping her face and kissing her forehead. "That's my girl."

"What can I do to help?" she asked.

"In the lab?" Francis said. "Nothing. Edgar and his team have it all under control. You can continue doing what you do so well... keeping me safe."

She made herself smile at him. "You're the boss."

CHAPTER 14

J udd stared silently at her. She could smell his horror and confusion and rested her hand on his thigh, squeezing gently. "You okay?"

"Am I okay?" He ran a hand through his hair before leaning against the headboard. "I just found out there's a fucking mad antelope shifter trying to sterilize the world, and you want to know if I'm okay?"

She nodded, and he sighed and rubbed Linda's belly when the dog nudged his hand. "I don't know how I feel."

He stiffened. "Wait, was it here? Was the lab here in Ashdale?"

"Yes," she said.

"Jesus fucking Christ." Fur sprouted across his body. "It's been six years. There's no way he hasn't used that machine to sterilize us. Hell, he's probably sterilized half the world by now."

"He hasn't," she said.

"You don't know that." Judd grew more and more agitated. "You have no idea if -"

"I do," she said. "Don't shift, okay?"

The fur faded, and his fangs retreated as he stared at her with sudden hope. "Tell me the thing those guys said you hid is that fucking machine."

"It is," she said.

"Thank Christ," he said. "How the fuck did you manage to take it?"

She sipped at her soda, her throat dry and scratchy from talking. "Even though I was the head of security, Francis had an entirely different security system for the lab. One I didn't have clearance for. It took me three months to devise a way to get into the lab."

"How did you do it?" he asked.

"I fucked Sam, one of the scientists on Edgar's team, then drugged him with a drug that would wipe his memory of the evening and stole his access card when he passed out," she said.

She waited for the judgment in Judd's eyes. Typically, she didn't give a fuck what anyone thought of her, especially when it came to whose bed she shared, but it was different with Judd. The idea that he might think less of her made her feel sick.

Instead of judgment, there was grudging respect. "Smart. So, you used his security card to break into the lab, took the machine, and hid it. What I don't understand is why Francis didn't just have the warlock make another when you took the first one."

"Because I killed Edgar," Tori said.

He grunted in surprise, and she took another sip of soda before staring at the far wall. "I chose a night when I knew Francis wouldn't be in the lab. He'd been spending nearly all of his free time at the office or in the lab, but he had a dinner that night with some diplomat from Europe. I knew he wouldn't miss it. I couldn't risk talking or flirting with Sam at the office, but I'd been watching him for the last few weeks and knew his habits. I showed up at the pub he went to every Friday night, flirted with him, and invited myself back to his place. Once I had his access card, breaking into the lab and getting my hands on the machine was surprisingly easy. It was getting out that proved nearly impossible."

———

Six years ago

"TORI, WHAT ARE YOU DOING BACK HERE SO LATE?" CRAIG, an affable elephant shifter who worked the security desk for their office building, smiled at her when she stepped out of the darkness and into the brightly lit lobby.

"Forgot my phone," she said.

He grinned and leaned back in his chair as she moved around the wide desk he sat at and leaned against the edge. "Fucking hate it when that happens."

"Tell me about it," she said. "I brought you a coffee."

"You're a damn angel." Craig removed the lid and sniffed at the dark liquid before taking a long sip. "Christ, that's good. Thanks, girl."

"Yeah, don't mention it." Behind her, multiple computer screens sat on Craig's desk, displaying various camera angles of the entire building, including the lab. She glanced casually at them. "Seems like a slow night."

"Nobody wants to work late on a Friday night. You got big plans for the weekend?"

"Not really. You?"

"Brook and I were thinking we might check out the new exhibit at -"

Craig's body went stiff before his eyes rolled up in his head, and he slumped toward the desk. Grimacing, Tori caught him and lowered the unconscious man to the floor behind the desk.

"Sorry, buddy." She squeezed his shoulder. "You'll be fine in a few hours, I promise."

She sat at his desk and quickly punched in her override code to shut down the security system, including the cameras. The screens went black, and she checked her watch. Four minutes until Francis got an email informing him of the security shutdown. Seventeen minutes before the security team of shifters she'd hired showed up to check the building for intruders.

Unless he calls the police, then you've got seven, maybe eight minutes, max.

She ran to the stairwell and started down the stairs to the lab. Francis wouldn't call the police. The last thing he wanted was law enforcement sniffing around the lab. No, he would call Tori first, and when she didn't answer, he'd send the entire team.

Her bunny thumping excitedly, Tori swiped Sam's card at the lab doors. The light stayed red, and muttering a curse, she flipped the card and swiped it again. The light turned green, and the door clicked. Her heart pounding, she opened the door and ran through the maze of hallways as her phone buzzed in her pocket.

She didn't bother looking. She knew it was Francis. She used Sam's card three more times before getting to the central lab. She swiped Sam's card a final time, more relief tumbling through her when the light switched to green and the door unlocked.

She slipped inside the dark room. She grabbed her phone, ignoring the missed call messages from Francis and studying the time. Fifteen minutes to destroy the serum and the machine and get the fuck out of the building. She'd call Francis as soon as she was a respectable distance from the building, tell him she was on her way to check out the situation, and he'd never know it was her.

The drug she'd used on both Sam and Craig would wipe their memories of tonight, and with the cameras disabled, there'd be no proof she was in the lab, but it didn't mean she wasn't fucking terrified that Francis would find out it was her.

He'll just build it again. He'll make the serum and the machine again, and there's only one way to stop him. You have to kill him.

She froze on her way toward the coolers, her heart stuttering, her bunny thumping, and her stomach ready to vomit the little food she'd managed to eat today.

She couldn't do that. Not to her Francis.

He isn't your Francis anymore. You think he wouldn't kill you if he found out you were doing this?

No, he wouldn't. Was he making a wrong decision based on fear? Yes, and she would convince him there were other ways than forced sterilization once she'd destroyed the serum and the machine. He was stubborn, and he might not listen. But he wouldn't kill her. He loved her as she loved him.

She shut out the voice in her head that wanted to keep arguing. She was wasting valuable time. Using her flashlight on her phone, she made her way to the cooler, opened the door and shone the light on the vials of purple serum.

The overhead lights blinked on, and dread crept into her stomach. She twisted around to stare at the man standing in the doorway.

"Hello, Astoria."

"Hello, Edgar." She pulled her gun from the holster around her waist and pointed it at him.

He shook his head. "You won't need that. I'm not going to stop you."

"Bullshit," she said.

Her heart raced, and fear seeped into her bones despite keeping a neutral look. She was fast, and she was strong, but she was no match for a fucking warlock.

"It's true," he said. "You're not the only one who believes Francis needs to be stopped."

"You created the serum and the machine," she said. "And now you're just going to destroy it? Why?"

"Does it matter?" he asked. "I've seen the error of my ways. What Francis - what *we* - are trying to do is wrong."

"Don't fucking move," she said as he approached her.

He stopped and held up his hands. "There's no point in wasting time destroying the serum. Francis has the formula, and the spell I used with the formula is easy enough for a competent witch or warlock to do. It's the machine we need to destroy. Without me, he won't be able to build it again, and I don't know about you, but I plan on leaving the country tonight and living on a nice isolated beach where Francis will never find me."

"Back up," she said.

He backed away from the steel table where the gray box sat at the center of it. Still holding the gun on him, Tori approached the table and studied the machine before reaching out with her free hand and running her fingers along the top.

"It's capable of spreading the serum across the city," Edgar said. "I finished the modifications last week. We're not finished with human trials, but Francis doesn't care. He's planning on using the machine in a few days."

"Where is he setting it off?" she asked.

"We're wasting time." Edgar glanced at the clock on the wall. "You've shut off the cameras, and it's alerted Francis. They'll be here soon."

"You're right," she said. Hoping she could trust him, but not having much choice, she holstered her gun and reached for the machine, lifting it high over her head."

"Wait, that won't -"

She smashed it onto the floor, her bunny thumping with surprise and a gasp escaping her throat when the box didn't break. She grabbed it and dropped it again before stomping on it with her foot. "What the fuck?"

"There's a protection spell around it. A very powerful one," Edgar said.

"You did it?" she asked.

He nodded. "Francis insisted. I need to break the spell before we can break the machine."

He picked up the machine and set it on the table. Tori glanced at her watch. "How long will this take?"

"Longer than I'd like," he said. "Be quiet. I need to concentrate."

She shut her mouth, pacing behind him as Edgar held his hands over the device. Her bunny thumped in alarm, and goosebumps broke out across her body as he spoke the incantation in a sing-song rhythm.

She watched silently as soft blue light glowed from Edgar's hands. He spoke louder and faster, and she glanced up when the overhead lights flickered. After nearly two minutes, she made a sound of impatience. "You need to hurry up."

"It's not that fucking simple," he said through gritted teeth. Sweat drenched his face, and his hands shook. "The spell is powerful."

"You're the one who created it," she said. "It should be simple for you to break it."

He swung around to face her. "Well, it's fucking not, and _"

His eyes widened, and she grunted in surprise when he pushed her hard to the right. She landed on her ass with a painful thud as gunfire rang out. She scrambled to her feet, her ears ringing, staring at Edgar as he touched his chest.

"Edgar," she said as red bloomed on the front of his shirt.

"Stop him," he said before collapsing.

She turned toward the door as Francis, holding a gun in his right hand, sighed loudly. "I didn't want it to be you, Astoria."

"What are you doing here?" she said through numb lips.

"I left my dinner as soon as I got the alert about the security cameras," he said. "You didn't think I would ignore it, did you?"

"You have a security team," she said.

"That I do. Of which you are the head of," Francis said. "Don't worry. The team is on their way. They'll be here any minute. Half of them, anyway. The others are at your place, on my orders. I was worried when you didn't answer my call."

He stepped into the room, studying Edgar lying on the floor before returning his gaze to Tori. "I told myself it wasn't you. I'd almost convinced myself, even though I knew you were lying about supporting my plan."

"Francis, you've gone insane," she said.

He laughed. "Insane? The planet is dying because people won't stop fucking and breeding, but I'm the insane one? I'm doing this for us, Tori. For you and your future children!"

"I won't have any children if you sterilize the fucking planet!" she snapped.

He shook his head. "Don't do that. You know everyone won't be sterilized. You'll still have your chance to breed."

"You can't do this, Francis."

"I can, and I will," he said.

She stood in front of the machine. "I can't let you do this."

His look of genuine sorrow almost broke her heart. "Then you leave me no choice."

He raised the gun again, and she swallowed hard. "You'll kill me? Is that it? You're the only father I've ever known, and now you're going to kill me?"

For a moment, she saw a flicker of the Francis he used to be. The hope rising in her died a cruel death when Francis's finger tightened on the trigger. "Goodbye, Astoria."

She cried out when a beam of green light hit Francis in the chest. He flew backward, crashing into the wall before slumping to the ground.

She knelt next to Edgar as the light faded from his hands, and he fell back with a harsh grunt. Blood dripped from his mouth, and he stared up at her, his hands clutching weakly at her shirt. "Go, you have to go."

"C'mon," she said, sliding her hands under his back and hauling him into a sitting position.

He cried out, and more blood flowed from his mouth. Blood soaked the front of his shirt, and he shook his head before clutching weakly at her shirt. "Have to go. They'll be here soon."

"I know," she said. "So get on your fucking feet. I'm not leaving without you."

"Can't," he gasped, "Take it and go. Destroy it."

"You can make it," she said. "I just need you to get up."

He laughed, more blood bubbling between his lips to drip down his chin. "Dying."

"I need you," she said.

"Find another to," he sucked in a gasp of air, "break the spell."

"Edgar, don't you fucking die on me," she said as he took another gasping breath before his body went limp. "Edgar!"

She shook him, but she didn't need to be a fucking doctor to know he was dead. She let him go and stared at the unconscious Francis, her hand reaching for the gun at her waist. She stood over him and aimed the gun at his head.

It's the only way to stop him. Do it.

"Tori?"

She spun around, staring wildly at Rick, who stood in the doorway with his gun drawn.

"What the fuck? Are you about to kill Francis?"

She shot Rick in the shoulder, wincing when he slammed into the wall, and a bellow of pain escaped his mouth.

"What the actual fuck!" he snarled as black and white striped hair sprouted on his face.

She ran across the lab, knocking Rick's gun from his hand when he raised it.

He cringed and said, "Tori, don't kill me."

She kicked his gun away before snatching the machine from the table and pointing the gun at Francis again.

"What are you doing?" Rick asked. "Tori, what the fuck is going on?"

"He has to be stopped," she said.

"By killing him? He's your friend," Rick said.

Her lower lip quivered, and she lowered the gun before sprinting out of the lab with the machine tucked under her arm. She heard footsteps running down the corridor and darted around the corner. She wasn't as fast in her human form as her bunny form, but she could still fucking move when needed, and she ran full out toward the doors at the far end of the hallway.

She pushed through them and headed for the stairwell, the only sound was her thundering heartbeat and Francis's voice echoing in her head.

CHAPTER 15

"You didn't kill Edgar. Francis killed him." Judd paced back and forth in the motel room, Linda at his heels.

"Francis was trying to kill me and killed Edgar instead. That's my fault," Tori said.

"No, it isn't," Judd said. "You're not a killer, Tori."

She hugged her knees to her chest, staring at him from her spot on the bed. "We both know that it isn't true, Judd. You saw exactly what I was last night."

He ran a hand through his hair. "You were defending yourself. There's a difference."

"Is there?" she asked.

"Yes," he said. "You didn't kill Francis that night."

"I should have," she said bitterly. "But I was weak."

"That wasn't weakness," he said. "You couldn't find a witch or warlock to break the protection spell on the machine?"

"No. But I didn't have a whole lot of time to find one. Francis was hunting me, and he has a lot of connections in the city. I was almost caught three times with the device before I finally hid the fucking thing, had an amnesia spell placed on me, and got the fuck out of the city."

Judd stopped so quickly that Linda ran into the back of his legs. "What about your family? Did Francis go after them?"

"I took a page from Francis's book and had a protection spell put on them."

"All of them?"

She nodded, and he let out a low whistle. "I didn't even know that was possible."

"The witch used my DNA as part of the spell. Anyone with my DNA is protected," Tori said. "Half siblings only share about twenty-five percent of their DNA, but it was enough."

"Christ, that must have cost a pretty penny," Judd said.

"All of my life savings," Tori said. "But I had to do it. I knew Francis would go after them to force me to bring him the device, and he did. Thanks to the protection spell, he failed.

"How long does it last?" Judd asked.

"Ten years. After that, I have to... renew it, I guess you'd say." Tori laughed, but it had a hollow sound that made Judd's chest ache.

"Where did you go when you left here?" Judd asked.

"Winchester," Tori said. "It wasn't far enough. Francis found me, and I almost died getting away."

Nausea infused Judd's body, and Linda, sensing his distress, whined softly and pawed at his shin. He picked her up, petting her soft fur. "Exactly how close did you come to dying, Tori?"

She picked at the quilt on the bed. "It was a long time ago, and it doesn't matter now - I survived. After that, I left the country. I bounced around Asia for a while and then moved to Europe. I ended up in Italy. I lived there until…."

"Until what?"

"Until Tamatha and Dan died."

The grief on her face had him hurrying to the bed. He sat beside her, dumping Linda on the mattress, and took Tori's hand. "I'm sorry, baby."

She smiled at him, rubbing her thumb over his knuckles. "Thank you."

"Tamatha and Dan… you mentioned them earlier," he said.

She nodded. "Tamatha and Dan were brown bear shifters. I went to school with their cub, Amos. They had him later in life. Dan was fifty-two when Amos was born, and Tamatha was in her late forties. He was their miracle baby. Amos and I were best friends, and I spent a lot of time at their farm. It was quiet at their place, and Tamatha and Dan were loving and kind. Not that my mom wasn't, but she had a lot of kits and an obsession with my dead father. It didn't leave her much time for one-on-one with her kits, and our house was always chaotic. Amos and his parents were important to me, and I stayed close to them until the shit with Francis went down."

"Francis didn't go after them?" Judd asked.

A small smile crossed Tori's face. "He tried. I couldn't tell my mom or my siblings they were in danger. They aren't fighters, and all of them are prey animals. Knowing they were in danger would have just frightened them. But Amos… he's as big as you, powerful, and always itching for a fight. I didn't give him all the details, just told him that Francis had lost his fucking mind and was out for my blood, and I had to disappear for a while. I warned him that Francis might use them to get to me. That was all he needed to know. He was living with his parents on their farm, and eventually, Francis sent shifters after them. It didn't go well for Francis's goons."

"That was it? Francis only tried once?" Judd said.

She nodded, her thumb still circling his knuckles. "Yes. Amos sent what was left of Francis's men to him in a plastic container with a note that there wouldn't be enough of Francis left to fit in a container if he went near him or his parents again."

Judd could smell her admiration and affection for Amos, and annoying jealousy reared its head. He cleared his throat. "Sounds like you and Amos were pretty close."

She studied him with her head cocked before dropping his hand and reaching for her phone on the nightstand. She scrolled across her screen and showed him a picture of a big Black man with a generous smile. "This is Amos, and this," she swiped to the following picture of Amos with his arm around a smaller Asian man who held a boy of about three on his hip, "is Amos's husband, Min-jun and their son Jamal."

His face reddening, Judd said, "They look happy."

She grinned at them. "They're very happy, my jealous bear."

He couldn't even deny that he'd been jealous. Not when she could smell it radiating from him like a potent spice.

He took her hand again, squeezing it lightly. "What happened to Dan and Tamatha?"

"Car accident," she said. "Amos rarely contacted me, it was too dangerous, but he knew I'd want to know."

"You came back for their funerals," he said.

She nodded. "I did. Amos told me not to and that his parents would understand, but I needed to be there. I wasn't stupid - I knew I couldn't go to the service, but I went to the gravesite after the service. I hid in the fucking trees and watched as they lowered two people I loved into the cold ground."

She didn't cry, Judd had an idea that it took a fuck of a lot to make Tori cry, but her voice had gone hoarse, and she was so pale, she looked nearly translucent. Without speaking, he put his arm around her waist and lifted her into his lap.

She rested her cheek on his chest, clinging to him as he rubbed her back and kissed the top of her head. "I'm so sorry, baby."

"Thank you," she said. "After the funeral, I told myself to leave. Ashdale is a big city, but it was still dangerous to be here. But I couldn't do it. I stayed a few days in a cheap motel, which turned into a few weeks. I couldn't talk to my mom or siblings, but I could," she paused, "check in on them. I hid in the park across the street and watched my mom as she gardened."

"I get it," Judd said. "Loneliness is a fucking bitch."

"Yeah," she said. "I was running out of money, so I applied at Bud's Bar. It was on the far side of the city from where Francis worked and lived and not an establishment that he would have set foot in anyway."

She sighed and rubbed at her forehead. "I shouldn't have stayed. I know that, but I…."

She hit herself on the thigh with a closed fist hard enough to make her slender body rock against Judd's. He grabbed her fist before she could punch herself again. "Don't, baby."

"If I hadn't stayed, you wouldn't be caught up in this fucking nightmare," she said.

He shrugged. "I also would have never met you."

She studied him, "Judd, we can't -"

"Where did you hide the machine?" He sure as fuck didn't want to hear what she was about to say.

"On Dan and Tamatha's farm."

135

"Seriously? That wouldn't be the first place Francis might look?"

"It's why I hid it there," she said. "It was the last place Francis would look because he'd assume I was too fucking smart to hide it on their farm."

Judd grunted out a laugh. "Makes sense. Sort of."

"I didn't tell Amos or his parents that I hid it there, and once the witch cast the amnesia spell, I didn't remember anyway."

"So, what's your plan?"

"Once Elora figures out how to break the protection spell, I'll destroy the machine," she said.

"And if she can't figure it out?" Judd asked.

"She will," Tori spoke confidently, but Judd could smell her doubt.

"That won't be enough to stop him," Judd said. "Even if you can destroy his machine, sooner or later, he'll find another witch powerful enough to create a new one."

"I know," she said. "After I destroy the machine, I'll kill Francis."

His bear whined at the coldness in Tori's voice. "Or you could take the machine to the police. Tell them what Francis is trying to do."

"Like they'd believe me," she said. "I'd have to get some of the serum as proof, and I don't particularly feel like breaking into Francis's lab again."

"I know some people who might be able to help us," Judd said.

"Us?" she said. "There's no us in this, Judd. You're staying right here at the motel while I fix this fucking mess."

"You honestly think I'm going to sit here on my ass while you try to stop a madman from sterilizing the city?" Judd said.

"Yes," Tori said.

Judd couldn't help but laugh. "Not happening, Tori-girl."

"Judd -"

"No," he said. "This isn't even a discussion. We're in this together now. You're stuck with me whether you like it or not."

She cupped his face. "If you get hurt, I…."

"I won't," he said.

"You might."

"I could get hurt crossing the street," he said.

She sighed, and when he saw she was about to argue again, he said, "Why did you fuck me?"

Her hand tightened on his face before she dropped it. "You know why. You could smell my lust for you every night in the bar, Judd."

"Just like you could smell mine. But why now? You've been stopping yourself for months from fucking me."

She looked away, studying Linda, who had fallen asleep on one of the pillows. "My bunny loves to fight, and she was amped up from it. When she's like that, she wants to fuck. You happened to be there and willing."

"So, that's it, huh? I was a warm and willing body, and nothing else?"

"Nothing else," she said before sliding off his lap. Without looking at him, she walked toward the bathroom. "We're both exhausted and need some sleep."

CHAPTER 16

She wanted to wake up. She wanted out of this hellish nightmare where she watched Judd torn apart repeatedly, but the dream was thick like molasses. No matter how hard she waded through it, she couldn't escape. She was doomed to watch her mate die until she and her bunny went mad. Until they -

"Wake up, Tori-girl."

His warm and familiar voice washed away some of the stickiness of her dream. She reached for his hand, wildly flailing until she felt the rasp of his palm against hers. "Judd, help me. I can't get to you."

"I'm here, baby. Open your eyes."

She blinked rapidly, shuddering her way out of the dream with the determination of a rabbit trapped in a cage.

"Wake up, baby."

She opened her eyes, staring at Judd, who sat on her bed in a pair of shorts. Linda was curled up on the extra pillow on Judd's bed, staring silently at them with her dark eyes before she yawned and closed her eyes.

"Judd?" Tori sat up and threw her arms around him. "Are you okay?"

"I'm fine, baby. You had a bad dream." Judd held her close, his big body rocking slightly.

After a few minutes, she leaned back to stare at him. "I'm sorry I woke you."

"It's okay." He smoothed her hair back.

"What time is it?"

"Almost seven. Are you getting hungry? We can order some dinner."

"I'm not hungry," she said and kissed him.

He returned her kiss, their tongues touching delicately before her common sense kicked in. She pulled back, making her bunny thump with genuine anger. "I shouldn't have done that."

"Why?" he asked.

"Because I don't want to give you the wrong idea."

"That you want to fuck me?" he asked with a raised eyebrow.

"That it could be something more. It can't, Judd."

"Why not?" he asked.

"Because…" She couldn't think of a solid reason, not when Judd was so close to her, and she could see his erection straining against his shorts.

He grinned at her. "How about while you're thinking about why we can't be anything more than fuck buddies, we fuck?"

"It's not a good idea," she said.

"I know what this is, Tori-girl," he said, "and I'm fine with it."

She pushed away the hurt and the doubt. It was good that Judd didn't want more because she didn't want more, either.

He pressed a kiss against her mouth, and she didn't pull

away this time. Instead, she climbed into his lap, straddling him and rubbing her pussy against his erection as he cupped her breast through her tank top.

Judd kissed her like he had all the time in the world. Kissed her until her lips were swollen, her breasts were heavy and tight, and her pussy was soaked. He rubbed at her nipple through her shirt until she couldn't take the teasing and yanked her shirt over her head. He made a low growl of appreciation at her naked breasts before bending his head and kissing a slow path to one dark pink nipple.

He kissed the tip of her nipple almost reverently before he sucked lightly on it. She moaned and threaded her hands through his thick dark hair, arching her back and rocking her pussy against his dick.

He growled again. She could feel the sound vibrating against her nipple, and why the fuck was that such a turn-on?

One big hand stroked her bare thigh, and he lifted his head to stare at her as he slid his hand into her shorts and cupped her mound. "So wet. Is this for me, Tori-girl?"

She nodded, squirming against his hand when his fingers grazed her clit. He slid his free arm around her waist and lifted her. "Take them off."

She yanked her shorts down, muttering in frustration when they got caught on her thighs. Judd laughed and, still holding her, stood and dropped her on her back on the bed.

He yanked her shorts off and tossed them to the floor before stretching between her legs, his big shoulders forcing her thighs wide. He kissed her inner thigh, his beard tickling her skin and making her shiver in all the right ways.

"You good with me eating your pussy?" He kissed her thigh again.

"Is there a woman out there who wouldn't be?" she asked.

He grinned at her. "Consent is important."

"It is," she said. "Does that mean I should ask you whenever I want to suck your dick?"

He growled and chuffed, his hands tightening around her legs. "Let's say you have blanket consent to suck my dick whenever you want, baby."

"Ditto for pussy eating, big guy," she said.

He growled again before burying his face in her pussy. She cried out and grabbed at his head, grinding herself against his face, against the delicious sensation of his mouth, tongue, and beard. He didn't tease or torment, although she had a feeling that next time she might not be so lucky, and she nearly arched off the bed when he sucked on her clit and slid one thick finger into her tight entrance.

"I love how wet you get, baby." He lifted his head, his beard wet and his lips shiny. "You taste so fucking sweet."

"Judd," she gasped. "Please. I was so close."

He fucked her with his fingers, watching her face as she moaned and squirmed and pleaded some more. Finally, with a soft smile, he gave her what she wanted.

His lips wrapped around her clit and sucked hard while two thick fingers worked in and out of her sopping pussy. With a harsh cry, she found her bliss, pounding her feet against the bed and squeezing Judd's head with her thighs.

He pried them apart, cleaning her pussy lips with his tongue and easing his fingers out of her pussy. "Fuck, I love the way you squeeze when you come. I can't wait to feel it on my dick again, Tori-girl."

"Then stop the talking and start the fucking, handsome," she said breathlessly as her body twitched and shook through the last of her orgasm.

He took off his shorts, and she sat up, admiring his gorgeous cock before reaching for it. He hissed in a breath when she wrapped her hand around his shaft and ran her thumb through the precum that coated the tip.

He knocked her hand away, and she pouted at him. "I want a taste."

"Fuck," he muttered before gently pushing her onto her back and kneeling between her thighs. "Next time, baby. I can't wait."

"This won't work," she said.

He immediately moved away to sit on the side of the bed. "Okay."

She grabbed his hand when he started to stand. "Hey, where are you going?"

"You said it wouldn't work," he said.

"Christ, I didn't mean for you to stop. I meant missionary wouldn't work," she said. "You're a damn giant compared to me, and I don't want my face slamming into your sternum while you're fucking me."

Relief poured into his face, and even though it was mean of her, she couldn't help but giggle. "You really thought I wouldn't give you an orgasm, too?"

He shrugged. "If you're not into it, I'm not into it. I can finish myself off in the shower."

"That is both the sweetest and the most fucked up thing I've ever heard," she said as she climbed back into his lap.

He groaned when her pussy brushed against his weeping dick. "Tori, baby, I need…."

"I know exactly what you need," she said, gripping his dick. "Help me take this monster dick, big guy."

He grunted out a laugh as his arm slid around her waist and lifted her. "It's average size for a bear."

She guided his average size for a bear dick to her waiting pussy. "It's huge and perfect."

He groaned as he lowered her onto his dick. She bit her

lip at the delicious stretch and burn, squeezing his shoulders with her hands when he finally sat fully in her. "Fuck, Judd, average sized or not, I am fucking stuffed full of dick."

He made a half-laugh, half-growl as he gripped her hips. "Am I hurting you?"

"No," she said. "I just need a minute."

His hands tightened on her hips as worry washed over his face. "Shit, did I hurt you last night? I didn't wait or -"

She kissed him, sucking lightly on his bottom lip before breathing against his mouth, "You didn't hurt me, Judd. In fact, I think I might be addicted to your dick already."

He huffed out a laugh. "I *know* I'm addicted to your sweet-tasting pussy."

"You can eat it whenever you want," she promised as she made an experimental bounce.

He groaned and made a shallow thrust. "Tori-girl, you feel so fucking good."

She nuzzled his neck and ran her thumb over his flat nipple before tugging on the barbell. He growled, his arm tightening around her, and she squealed when he made two hard, deep thrusts.

"You like that, huh?" she said before tugging on his second barbell.

"Fuck!" The word exploded from his mouth like a prayer as he held her tight and fucked her hard.

She rode his thrusts, kissing him deeply as she played with the barbells until he growled and groaned.

She leaned back, and he splayed one big hand across her back to hold her steady as they watched her pussy take his dick. There was something a little obscene and entirely satisfying seeing his flushed red dick and the pink of her inner pussy as she took each thrust, her swollen lips clinging to his wet cock.

"Can you come again for me, baby?" he groaned.

"If you're cool with me touching myself," she panted.

"Whatever gets you off," he said.

She scored him another mental point before rubbing her clit with tight, fast circles that pushed her right to the edge almost immediately.

"I'm gonna come," she moaned.

"Yes," he said. "Fuck, yes."

She rubbed harder, her pussy clamping around Judd's dick when that exquisite pleasure washed over her. Judd bellowed her name, yanking her against his chest and burying his face in her neck as he emptied himself into her. She could feel his pulsing heat against her inner walls as he pumped into her.

With a shuddering growl, he collapsed on his back on the bed. She grinned down at him, enjoying the feel of his softening cock inside her. Hell, she even enjoyed the feel of his cum already started to drip out of her.

"That was fucking incredible," he mumbled.

She gave him a pleased look. "I'm pretty sure you gave me a swimming pool's worth of cum."

His cheeks turned pink and holy hell, until this moment, she didn't think Judd could be any hotter. "You're blushing."

He cleared his throat, his big hands rubbing her hips. "I don't usually have sex without a condom. My tests are negative."

"Mine are, too," she said. "But I know what most shifters think about bunnies and their love of fucking, so I'm happy to show you proof."

"No." He squeezed her hips. "I trust you."

She really should get off Judd, he had softened completely, and things were getting very sticky down there, but she stayed where she was, waiting for him to ask her about birth control.

When he didn't, she said, "Don't you want to know if I'm on birth control?"

"I assumed you were," he said.

"You know what assuming does," she said.

He stayed utterly relaxed beneath her, like the idea that she might get pregnant with his cub didn't bother him. "Are you on birth control?"

"I am," she said.

"Then we're good," he said.

"We are." She ran her fingers over one of his barbells before giving it a light tug. His cock twitched inside of her, and she grinned at him. "Did you get your nipples pierced because it makes you come when they're touched?"

He laughed. "No. My nipples being more sensitive from the piercing was a happy surprise."

"Now I know why you're so anxious to keep them," she said teasingly.

He laughed again before reaching up to cup her small breast. "Maybe you should pierce your nipples and see if it makes them more sensitive."

"They're sensitive enough," she said as he sat up and kissed the tip of one.

"You did seem to like it when I sucked on them." He pulled her nipple with his lips.

She shivered, lust reigniting in her belly just like that. "You're as insatiable as a bunny, my handsome bear."

"I am," he agreed before nuzzling her neck. "Want to fuck in the shower before we order dinner?"

"Yes, I believe I would," she said.

He laughed and stood up, holding her against him as he carried her to the bathroom.

CHAPTER 17

"Hey, you okay?" Hudson ducked into the motel room.

"Yeah, I'm good," Judd said.

"What the fuck is going on? You call in sick tonight and text me asking me to come here after my shift. Why aren't you at home?" Hudson bent and picked up Linda when she rested her paws on his shin and barked.

"It's a long story," Judd said.

"It's two in the morning. Where the fuck else do I have to be?" Hudson said.

"You didn't tell Rosalie you were coming here, did you?"

Hudson shook his head, but his face darkened. "I haven't yet because you asked me not to, but you need to know that I won't keep secrets from my mate. Not when I almost lost her because of it."

"I know, and I wouldn't ask you to if it wasn't -"

The bathroom door opened, and Hudson groaned when Tori stepped into the room. "Fuck me. What is she doing here?"

"What the fuck are *you* doing here?" Tori asked.

Linda squirmed to be released, and Hudson set her down.

She ran across the room to Tori, who scooped her up and let her lick her face before petting her gently.

"What the hell is going on?" Hudson said.

"It's none of your fucking business," Tori said, her voice cold. "Leave."

"And if I don't?" Hudson growled at her.

"I'll make you leave," she said. Her voice still cold and steady, she stared unblinkingly at the polar bear shifter.

Judd released his breath in a harsh rush when Hudson's body relaxed, and he grinned at Tori. "I like this version of Tori a fuck of a lot more than the dumb bunny version."

She rolled her eyes before turning to Judd. "Why did you call him?"

"Because we can't do this alone. Not if we want to break into the lab and get some of that serum as proof."

"You're putting him in danger, Judd."

Hudson crossed his arms over his chest. "Judd's my best friend, and he nearly died for me. Whatever he needs from me, he'll get it."

"You almost died?" Tori stared at Judd.

"It doesn't matter. I survived," Judd said, echoing her words from earlier.

She frowned at him as Hudson growled with impatience. "Tell me what the fuck is going on, Judd."

"Sit down," Judd said. "It's a long fucking story."

"WE'LL NEED MORE PEOPLE THAN JUST YOU AND ME TO break into the lab," Hudson said.

Tori stared at him from where she sat perched on the desk. "That's it? A madman is trying to sterilize the city, and you have nothing to say about that?"

"What is there to say?" Hudson asked. "He needs to be stopped, and we need proof for anyone to believe us. We've got the device, but that doesn't mean shit without the serum. So, we steal some of the serum and take it and the device to the police. Have you heard from the witch about the protection spell?"

"Not yet," Judd said.

"What if she can't break it?" Hudson asked.

"She will," Tori said.

She sounded confident enough, but Judd suspected it was for Hudson's benefit.

"Will you talk to Mal and Bishop and Kat for me?" Judd asked. "They might be willing to help."

"They're not going to break the law," Tori said. "They're a reputable security firm, not vigilantes out for justice."

"I think when the fucking city is about to be sterilized, they'll make an exception for breaking the law," Hudson said.

"We may need a few of their employees too. Maybe Fenton, and," Judd paused, "Ronin."

"I hate that fucking bird," Hudson said with a sigh.

"Yeah, me too, but you have to admit he's good in a fight," Judd said.

"What if they don't believe you?" Tori asked suddenly.

"Why wouldn't they?" Hudson said.

"Oh, I don't know… maybe because an antelope shifter creating a way to sterilize nearly the entire fucking world is a bit of a stretch to believe?"

"They'll believe us," Judd said.

"You can't know that."

"I do," Judd said. "You need to trust me on this, Tori."

She picked at her fingernail. "What if they get hurt or die? Can you live with that, Judd? Can you live with the fact that you got your friends killed?"

"They aren't going to die," Judd said steadily. "Besides, what's the alternative? Even if we manage to destroy the device, who's to say Francis won't eventually find another witch to build it again? He needs to be stopped, Tori, and we need more than just the two of us to do it."

She bit at a hangnail on her thumb and didn't say anything. Judd turned back to Hudson. "Can you talk to them?"

"Yes," Hudson said. "I'm meeting with them about a job later today and I'll talk to them then."

"That's great, man." Judd clapped him on the back. "I'll miss you at the bar, but I'm happy for you."

"You want me to talk to Porter, too?" Hudson asked.

Judd glanced at Tori, who sighed but nodded. "Yeah, we can't both keep calling in sick."

Judd picked up Linda. "Can I ask one more favour? Can you keep Linda at your place for a little while? I want to keep her safe, and if Francis finds us again..."

"Sure. But if Mr. Pibbles claws my ass in retaliation for bringing a dog into the house, I'm sending you photographic evidence," Hudson said.

Judd grinned as Tori said, "Mr. Pibbles?"

"My mate's cat," Hudson said. "I'll call you after I've talked to Mal and the others."

"Thanks, man. I appreciate it." Judd held out his hand, grunting in surprise when Hudson hugged him.

Linda squirmed between them, and Hudson stepped back before picking up Linda's food. His throat weirdly tight, Judd dressed Linda in her jacket and held her up to his face. She licked his cheeks and chin, and telling himself this wouldn't be the last time he ever saw her, he kissed her furry forehead. "I'll see you soon, sweetheart. Be good for Hudson and Rosalie. Daddy loves you."

Hudson took Linda, and Judd cleared his throat. "She likes to sleep in your bed at night. I don't know if Rosalie will have a problem with that or …."

"Knowing my mate, she'll let Linda sleep on her pillow," Hudson said. "Rosalie loves animals, Judd."

"I know," he said. "Tell her thank you for me."

"I will. I'll call you soon."

Hudson left, and Judd shut the door. He took a deep breath, twitching a little when Tori's arms slid around his waist, and she kissed his back. "She'll be okay, big guy. Hudson will keep her safe."

"I know," he said.

"You'll see her again," she said, making him twitch again. Could she read his fucking mind?

She kissed his back a second time. "I won't let anything happen to you. I promise."

He turned in her arms, smoothing her hair back from her face. "I'm sorry I didn't tell you I texted Hudson, but we need him."

"I know," she said. "I'm glad you have him in your life. He's a good guy."

"He is," Judd said. "He's an even better friend."

She smiled, but the look on her face hurt Judd's heart. He pressed a kiss against her forehead. "I'm sorry you can't talk to Amos as often as you want."

She shook her head. "It's fine. I'm used to it now. I've been alone for a very long time."

He cupped her face, staring into her beautiful blue eyes. He hoped the emotion evident on his face - he wouldn't call it love, nope, it was too fucking soon for love no matter what his dumb heart told him - didn't scare her away. "You're not alone anymore, baby."

Tears glinted in her eyes for a moment. She blinked and

they were gone, and she ran her hand over his ass. "Are you tired, my bear? Or can I finally get my mouth on that average for a bear, fucking beautiful cock of yours?"

He growled, his dick automatically hardening at the thought of being in her mouth. "Baby, you can do whatever you want to me."

CHAPTER 18

Tori would never find anything sexier than Judd's low growls and groans, how his hand tightened in her hair, or the steady way he held her gaze as she sucked his magnificent cock.

She gripped the base of him, twisting her palm lightly back and forth as she circled the head with her tongue before cleaning away the precum that coated the tip.

"Tori," Judd moaned, "baby, you're fucking perfect."

She released him with a soft pop and went to work on his balls, lightly stroking them before sucking one into her mouth. He made a hoarse growl, his hand tightening painfully against her scalp. "Fuck! Baby, fuck!"

She lifted her head, stroking his thick thighs as she stared at him. His knee dug into her ribs, and she shifted on the bed, easing some pressure.

"Tori," Judd's voice was urgent as his palm pressed against the back of her head, trying to move her back to his dick, "I need more."

"Is that right?" She licked his dick from the base to the

tip, lingering at the slit on top, teasing it with her tongue until he made another harsh groan, and his hips rose from the bed.

She sucked him again, using plenty of spit and tongue. Her entire body throbbed for release. Getting Judd off was a sweet drug she never wanted to kick, but she kept her fingers away from her pussy. She wanted Judd's rough fingers on her clit, wanted him to touch her in the way she was already addicted to.

He was getting close. She could hear it in his low voice as he said her name repeatedly, punctuated with low groans and muttered pleas for mercy.

She released him, ignoring his growl of frustration. "Do you want to come in my mouth or my pussy?"

"Pussy," he said. "This time."

She kissed the short patch of pubic hair above his cock. "Pretty bold of you to assume I'll suck your dick again."

He grinned and ran his hand through her hair. "Baby, I plan on having your beautiful mouth around my dick every fucking night."

"Horny bastard," she said and nipped his hipbone.

"Like you're not just as horny as I am," he said.

She laughed. "You've got me there." She got onto her hands and knees, looking at Judd over her shoulder before wiggling her bare ass at him. He stared at her pussy, one big hand stroking his cock back and forth.

"You gonna just look at it or do something with it, big guy?" she asked.

"Do something," he said, moving to his knees behind her.

His hands smoothed across her ass, squeezing and stroking before he slipped his hand between her thighs. She reared up when he rubbed her pussy, leaning back against Judd when he dropped his free arm around her waist. He cupped one tiny breast, teasing her nipple as his fingers worked her clit. He kissed the back of her shoulder, groaning when she ground her ass against his cock.

"Judd, please," she said when he dipped two fingers into her pussy. "I need your dick."

"You don't like my fingers?" He teased her clit with his thumb as he slid his fingers in and out of her.

"I like your dick," she huffed before slapping at his arm. "Give me what I want."

"Yes, Tori-girl," he said with amusement in his voice. He bent her over again, gripping her shoulder as she clutched the quilt and tried not to beg.

She moaned when he slid into her, his cock stretching her in the most delicious of ways. He took his time, easing in and out until she thought she might scream with need and want and frustration.

When he was finally seated within her, she made a hoarse cry of pleasure, her pussy tightening around him. He groaned and squeezed her shoulder. "Baby, ease up. Christ, you're gonna make me come."

"I want you to come," she panted as she rocked her body back and forth. "I want you to give me everything, Judd."

"Soon," he groaned. He gripped her hip with his other hand and held her immobile. She thrilled in the power of his big body, her desire notching higher at being entirely at his mercy.

His to take, his to fuck, his to love.

She stiffened at that errant thought, and Judd stopped, his hand petting her lower back. "You okay, baby? Did I hurt you?"

"No," she said. "I'm good."

"You sure?" He caressed her spine, the roughness of his fingers making her wish they were back on her sensitive clit.

"Yes," she snapped. "Fuck me, Judd, before I lose my mind over here."

He chuckled and, thank fucking Christ, slid his hand under her to cup her mound. "Whatever you want, Tori-girl."

He gave her clit a few delicious strokes, just enough to get her motor revving, before gripping her hips and pounding into her. She took every stroke, her body begging for more, her pussy stuffed full, and her brain going blank as the pleasure soared.

He lifted her slightly and made a small change in position before fucking her again, and just like that, his beautiful, definitely not fucking average, cock was brushing against her G-spot with every hard thrust.

She screamed his name, not caring if anyone heard her, and clawed at the sheets. Her back arched, and she screamed again when she came in a roaring, twisting tsunami of pleasure. Judd roared, the sound echoing and bouncing in the small room and making her ears ring.

Someone pounded on the other side of the wall, hollered at them to 'shut the fuck up, already', as Judd came deep inside her, flooding her insides with warmth. She squeezed around him, her pussy milking the last of his cum out of him before she collapsed on her face.

Judd dropped to the mattress beside her, his shaking body vibrating the entire bed. Utterly spent, she rolled to face him, flinging one leg over his and resting her cheek on his chest. His heart thundered in her ear, and she could hear him panting and huffing like a wounded buffalo.

"You okay?" she asked.

"Yeah," he rasped. "We're gonna get a noise complaint."

She laughed weakly. "Probably. Worth it."

"So fucking worth it," he said before kissing her forehead.

It was nearly four in the morning, and exhaustion crept in. Tori wanted to lie there forever, but she forced herself to sit up, smiling at Judd when he grabbed her hand.

"Where are you going?"

"Bathroom," she said. "I need to pee and clean up."

He relaxed and let go of her hand, resting his forearm against his eyes as she headed to the bathroom.

When she returned, he was in his bed, and she hesitated briefly before climbing in beside him. He smiled without opening his eyes. "Hello, Tori-girl."

"Did you switch beds because of the wet spot or because you thought I didn't want you sleeping in my bed?" she asked.

"A little of both," he admitted. "Fuck buddies don't generally spend the night in each other's bed."

That niggle of hurt appeared again, and this time it was harder to ignore. Her bunny thumped, but she was more depressed than angry.

It's okay, sweet one.

Her bunny ignored her. She believed Judd was her mate, and Tori's refusal to get with the fucking program was beginning to cause a divide between them. That divide scared the shit out of Tori, if she was being honest. But what the fuck could she do about it? Judd didn't see her as anything more than a fun time, and she wouldn't beg him for more.

He said he was good with being fuck buddies because you told him you wanted that. Maybe he wants more. Have you even asked him?

No, and the intelligent and emotionally mature thing to do was sit down and have an honest discussion with him. But not now. Not when they were exhausted and after he'd just given her the best fucking orgasm of her life. She needed to be clearheaded for that particular conversation, and she was currently buzzed on dopamine.

"I like being in your bed," she said.

He pulled her close, tangling their legs together and rubbing her back with long slow strokes as he pressed a kiss against her mouth. "I like having you in my bed."

She closed her eyes, listening to Judd's breathing even out. Warm and relaxed, her bunny finally at peace in Judd's arms, she closed her eyes and slept.

TORI WATCHED IN AMUSEMENT AS JUDD PULLED BURGER after burger out of the to-go bag. Four burgers and two cartons of fries later, he handed her the salad she'd requested before unwrapping a burger and taking a huge bite.

"How much of your paycheque goes toward food?" She opened her salad and ate a bite.

"Hey, it's your fault I'm so hungry," he said.

She arched an eyebrow at him. "How is it my fault?"

"You made me skip breakfast. I never skip breakfast." He finished one burger and ate some fries before starting the next burger.

"We missed breakfast because we slept in and because someone wanted sex in the shower again," she said.

"I love shower sex," he said. "It's my favourite kind of sex."

She laughed. "So, your paycheque goes toward your water bill, is what you're saying."

He did that low laugh she loved. "Totally worth it."

Judd ate the rest of his food, cheerfully finishing the last of her salad when she offered it to him.

He wiped his mouth and drank some water before leaning against the headboard. "Hudson called me while I was out getting food."

She tensed, her bunny thumping nervously. "And?"

"They've agreed to help us. Kat's researching Francis's lab and the building schematics and security detail, and Bishop and Mal are formulating a plan for getting in there. Oh, and they posted someone outside the motel."

"What?" She slid off the bed, walked to the window, and peeked past the drawn curtains. She scanned the parking lot and the street. "Where are they?"

"The black Ford Escape," Hudson said. "Blond guy behind the wheel."

Her gaze narrowed in on the vehicle parked halfway down the street but with a good view of the motel and their room. A blond man sat behind the wheel, staring at his phone, but she didn't miss how he glanced up every thirty seconds to scan the area.

"His name's Fenton. He's a cheetah shifter. If Francis's men manage to find us here, he'll give us an early warning and provide backup if needed."

She returned to the bed and sat next to Judd. She picked at a hole in her jeans, trying to process the weird feeling inside her.

"You okay?" Judd rested one warm hand on her leg.

"Yeah, I feel…."

"Feel what?" He gave her an encouraging look.

"I don't know. Surprise… relief. It's the first time in a long time that I'm not alone, and I'm struggling to process it."

He squeezed her thigh. "I told you, baby, you'll never be alone again."

She took a deep breath. Now was the time to talk to Judd. He certainly looked at her like he wanted more than just sex, and he talked a lot about her never being alone again for someone who only wanted a fuck buddy.

"Judd, are you -"

Her phone rang, and she grimaced before grabbing it from the nightstand. Her stomach tensed, and her pulse picked up when she glanced at the screen. "It's Elora."

She answered the call and put it on speaker. "Hey, Elora. You're on speaker with Judd and me."

"Hi!" Excitement tinged the young witch's voice. "I think I know what kind of protection spell it is, and if I'm right, I should be able to break it."

"Holy shit," Judd said. "You serious right now?"

"As a heart attack," Elora said. "I couldn't find anything on the internet or in any of the modern spellbooks about the spell your warlock was using to break it. It's seriously old-school magic - both the protection spell and the breaking spell - but I finally found it in this ancient spellbook of my grandmother's that she had in storage."

"I could kiss you right now, little witch," Tori said.

Elora laughed again. "That's cool, but I'm straight. Although, if Lilianna doesn't stop cockblocking me, I might have to give the ladies a try."

Lilianna's loud and obnoxious caw made Tori's bunny thump and Judd growl under his breath.

"Okay, okay, Lilli-pad, cool it, jeesh," Elora said. "Anyway, I'm free this afternoon if you want to bring the object over, and I'll see if I'm right."

"See if you're right?" Judd said. "You just said you found the spell."

"No, I said I think I found the right spell. But I won't

know until I have the object in front of me and try to break the protection spell."

"It's not currently in my possession, but I'll have it by tonight and can bring it to you tomorrow," Tori said.

"Sure, that works," Elora said. "Around ten?"

"See you then," Tori said.

She ended the call, excitement and anxiety circling her stomach and making her regret eating the salad.

Judd took her hand. "I guess we're about to see your friend Amos."

She shook her head. "Amos sold the farm after his parents died. He and Min-jun live here in the city now."

"Where exactly is the device on the farm?" Judd asked.

"Under the barn. There are a few loose floorboards in one of the stalls."

"What if the new owners discovered the loose floorboards and the device? Or what if they tore down the barn?"

"There's only one way to find out," she said.

"So, we're just gonna knock on a stranger's door and ask them to let us hang out in their barn for a while?" Judd said.

"No. You'll stay here while I drive there and, under cover of darkness, break into their barn and grab the device."

"You're not doing any of this cloak-and-dagger spy shit without me," Judd said. "No arguing, Tori."

"I could just knock you out, tie you to the bed with zip ties, and leave," she said.

"You carry zip ties with you?"

"Doesn't everyone carry zip ties?" she asked.

He grinned and pulled her into his lap. "Or, while we're waiting for it to get dark, I could tie you to the bed with your zip ties. I'll eat your sweet pussy until you're coming all over my face, and the people in the room next to ours make another noise complaint. Then once it's dark, we'll drive to the farm and get that fucking device."

She rubbed her hand over his beard. "You make it very difficult to resist you, my bear."

He kissed her palm and cupped her breast, rubbing his thumb over her hardening nipple. "Probably best if you just stop resisting and let me eat your sweet pussy."

She grinned at him. "I'll get the zip ties."

CHAPTER 19

"Andrew, get your butt back here right now and help your sister and me with the groceries!"

"Aw, c'mon, Mom. Vanessa and the others will be here in fifteen minutes, and I gotta get the fire started."

"The car, now."

From his spot next to Tori in the woods surrounding the farmhouse, Judd grinned when Andrew muttered a curse and stomped back toward the car like he was walking to his own beheading.

The farm was a few miles outside town, past Hayes River, and a few miles into Parsons Woods. They'd driven to the farm at dusk, parking a few miles away on a snowy side road and hiking through the woods. By the time they stood at the edge of the woods, darkness had fallen, but a car was pulling into the driveway.

Judd sniffed the air. The mother and her children were squirrel shifters, and he and Tori both shrank back into the trees when the mother stopped and turned in their direction, sniffing rapidly.

Squirrels had an incredible sense of smell, and Judd held his breath when the mom took a few steps toward the woods, her nose twitching and her petite body tense. There was no way she couldn't smell his scent, but he just had to hope she thought it was an actual bear. Beside him, Tori was stiff and tense, and when she slipped her hand into his, he gripped it tightly.

"Mom!" The little girl, who looked about ten and tiny even for a squirrel shifter, ran up to her.

"What's wrong, Mari?" The mother continued to stare into the trees.

"Andrew says I can't hang out at the bonfire tonight." Mari grabbed her mother's hand, squeezing it until she looked down. "Tell him I'm allowed."

"It's for my friends," Andrew hollered from the car as he loaded himself down with multiple bags of groceries. "Not for stupid little sisters who smell like pinecones."

"I don't smell like pinecones!" Mari shrieked so loudly that Judd's bear growled.

"Yes, you do, nut breath," Andrew said.

"Mo-om!" Mari shouted.

"Enough! Both of you!" Their mother rubbed wearily at her forehead. "Mari, you may join them for an hour at the bonfire."

"What?" Andrew and Mari said simultaneously.

"Only an hour? Why can't I stay two hours?"

"She can stay for fifteen minutes," Andrew said.

"I can stay an hour, Andrew! Mom already said. Besides, it's not like Vanessa's gonna make out with you like you're hoping. She isn't attracted to your bushy ass."

Tori snorted before clamping her free hand over her mouth as her body shook with laughter.

"My ass isn't bushy!" Whiskers sprouted from Andrew's face as his front teeth lengthened, and he chittered angrily.

"Enough!" their mother snapped. "Seriously, you two, if you don't stop fighting, I'm sending you to stay with your father for the week. He won't put up with your bullshit the way I do."

Still holding Mari's hand, she returned to the car, grabbing a bag of groceries and handing them to Mari. "Take this into the house. Andrew, I'll get the last two bags. Take the groceries inside before your friends arrive."

The three squirrel shifters walked into the farmhouse, and Judd released his breath. "We need to get into that barn and be quick." He sniffed in the direction of the barn. "I don't smell any animals in it."

"You stay here," Tori said. "I'm faster and quieter than you."

"I'm not letting you go in there alone," he said.

"It's an empty barn, Judd, not a war zone," Tori said. "I'll be back in five minutes."

"Too late," Judd said as a second car pulled into the driveway, and a pile of teenagers climbed out. The light above the farmhouse door turned on, and bright light flooded the front yard.

"Shit," Tori muttered.

Andrew came out of the farmhouse, bumping fists and talking loudly to his friends as they headed toward the field beside the barn. They joked and harassed each other as they quickly built the bonfire. It illuminated the barn's front doors, and Tori muttered another curse.

"Looks like we're hanging out in the woods for a few hours," Judd said.

"Yeah." Tori checked her cell phone as the farmhouse

front door banged open, and Mari stepped outside. The little girl hurried toward the bonfire as Judd took off his jacket, placed it on the snow-covered ground at the base of a large tree and sat down on it. "C'mere, Tori-girl."

She joined him, and he tugged her into his lap. "No point in both of us sitting in the snow."

"You'll freeze to death. He wore a long-sleeved shirt, and she rubbed her hands over his shoulders and biceps."

"Nah, I'm warm-blooded. I'm no polar bear, but you know how we bears are. We all run hot. My ex used to sleep in the guest room when she stayed over. She said sleeping in my bed was like sleeping beside a furnace."

Tori leaned against him, running one small hand over his chest. "I like how warm you are. I get cold at night."

He grinned at her. "I'm happy to warm you up whenever you need it, doll."

He wrinkled his nose when the skunk smell drifted across the cold wind. Various other scents were mixed in… raccoon, fox, and deer, and although he had a highly attuned sense of smell, it was impossible to know if they were animals or shifters.

He stared into the darkness, but the world around them was quiet and still.

"Do you see anyone?" Tori asked.

He shook his head. "No, probably just animals, not shifters."

As the teenagers' laughter pierced the night air, Tori said, "Why did you and your ex break up?"

"She got a job in Mexico. She asked me to move there with her, but we'd only been dating a year and…."

"And?" she asked.

"I like my life here," he said. "My parents are here, and my brother is only a few hours away."

"You have a brother?" she asked.

"Yes. He's a few years younger than me. Anyway, it was a big commitment to move to a completely different country for a girl who hadn't even said she loved me."

"Seriously?"

"Yeah. She was a snow leopard, and you know how they are."

"Standoffish," Tori said. "They don't usually mate for life."

"They don't," Judd said. "I had the feeling she only asked me to move with her because I was something familiar to her, you know?"

"I do," she said. "Have you slept with a prey animal before me?"

I slept with a deer shifter once," Judd said.

"Nothing small, though?"

"No. Prey animals tend to avoid us."

He hesitated, and she gave him an encouraging look. "What?"

"A few of us at the bar were surprised by how often you slept with a predator shifter, but I guess that's the wolverine in you, huh?"

She smiled. "I guess. Does it bother you how many people I've fucked?"

He blinked at the bluntness of her question. "No, should it?"

"It's bothered previous partners," she said.

His stupid heart kicked it up a notch, and his bear growled happily at the word partner.

Knock it off. She doesn't mean anything by it.

Yes, she does! His bear turned pouty. *She is our mate.*

"It doesn't bother me," he said.

167

She studied him before cupping his face and kissing him. "Thanks, big guy."

She shivered delicately, and he wrapped his arms around her, pulling her against his chest as he leaned against the tree.

"Can I ask you another question?" Tori said.

"You can ask me as many as you want," he said.

"Why don't you work for the security firm? I know you pitch in here and there, but I also know that Bishop has asked you straight out to work full-time for them. You'd make a lot more money working for them."

"I've considered it a few times, and I'm not completely ruling it out, but I like being a bouncer," Judd said. "Porter pays a better wage than most bar owners, and I'm a night owl, so the hours appeal to me. Once I find my mate and we have cubs, depending on what she does for a living, I might have to find a higher-paying job. But for now, I make enough to support Linda and me just fine."

"How many cubs do you want?" she asked.

"Two or three. You?"

"Two is my max," she said. "How did you almost die for Hudson?"

He cleared his throat. His memory of how he survived that night was a little fuzzy, but he did his best to explain. "Hudson's mate, Rosalie, was taken by a grizzly bear shifter named Corden as bait to lure Hudson in. Corden's son John had murdered Hudson's friend Samuel. Hudson found Samuel's body, and then John showed up and tried to kill Hudson. Hudson killed him and his men, left Canada, and moved here to stay under the radar. If he'd stayed in Canada, Corden would have murdered him."

"I guess Hudson and me have some shit in common," Tori said.

"Yeah," Judd said. "Anyway, Corden held Rosalie hostage at a closed campground outside the city and told Hudson to meet him there. Me and Porter, and a bunch of others, including Mal, Bishop, and Kat, went with him as backup. Fucking good job we did, too, because Corden had a shit ton of shifters there. There was a giant ass battle, and I took on a couple of bears to give Hudson time to go after Corden, who tried to escape into the woods with Rosalie."

"Two against one," she said.

"Yeah. It didn't go well for me."

She rubbed his arms again, staring silently at him as he tried to figure out how to put into words what he'd felt that night. He'd never spoken about it before, not even to Hudson, and he could feel his throat tightening, and his bear made a low snarl that held more anxiety than anger.

"They slashed me wide open, broke my back, and paralyzed me," Judd said. "I was bleeding out, and I knew I was dying, but it didn't hurt, and I was afraid but not terrified, you know?"

She nodded. "I do."

"I was just glad that Hudson had got his girl back and that I was dying because of something… something noble and good."

She made a soft sound of comfort, her hands smoothing over his shoulders and back down his arms.

"My life was saved by…." He'd promised Mal and the others that he wouldn't tell anyone what Ronin was, but he didn't have to tell Tori it was Ronin. "A phoenix saved my life."

"Ronin," Tori said.

He jerked in surprise, staring wide-eyed at her. "How did you know?"

She shrugged. "I didn't know for certain, but I knew he was no ordinary bird. He's Kat's mate, and if she were there with you, he would be too."

"You can't tell anyone," Judd said. "If the wrong people find out he's a phoenix...."

"I won't say anything," she said. "Ronin's secret is safe with me."

"Thanks, baby."

"So, it must have really chapped your ass that Ronin saved your life, huh?"

He sighed deeply. "You have no fucking idea."

She laughed and kissed him. "Well, I, for one, am planning on buying Ronin a beer the next time I see him."

"He'd probably rather have a taco," Judd said.

She grinned. "I can do tacos."

She lapsed into silence, and he held her a little closer, listening to the faint sound of her breathing and the rapid beat of her heart. The ground was uncomfortable, and the Solum Winds felt like they were blowing right through him, but he enjoyed this moment with her. He wanted so much more from Tori than just her body, and even though he knew this meant more to him than her, knew that her questioning him about his life was just a way for her to pass the time, his bear was still giddy from happiness, and he couldn't help but absorb some of that happiness.

"Did you grow up in Ashdale?" Tori asked.

Another wave of happiness washed over him. Maybe this didn't mean anything to her, and maybe she'd forget every personal thing he told her tonight, but he would hold on to that flickering spark of hope deep in his chest that perhaps she wanted more.

"I'M SNEAKING INTO THE BARN," TORI SAID.

"They're still around the bonfire," Judd said.

Tori glanced at her watch. "We've been sitting here for five hours. The fire is low and not throwing off as much light."

Judd frowned. "They can still see the barn doors from the bonfire."

"I'm fast and quiet," she said. "I can get in and out without them noticing."

"And if you don't?" Judd asked. "They're a bunch of teenagers. It's not like you can beat the shit out of them."

She laughed. "I wouldn't beat up kids, Judd. They won't see me, I promise."

"I think we should wait." Judd peered around the tree, studying the teens and then the barn. "They'll leave, eventually."

Tori shook her head. "I'm nearly frozen, and I know you're cold too, even with your 'bear heat'. I'll grab the device, and we'll get the hell out of here."

"Tori -"

She stood on her tiptoes and kissed him. "Be right back, my bear."

He growled his disapproval, but she just winked at him before taking off through the trees toward the barn. His body shaking from cold and adrenaline, he watched as Tori sprinted out of the trees to the right side of the barn. She crept toward the corner of the barn and peeked around the edge, studying the doors and the teens around the bonfire.

His hands clenched into fists, and his bear made a disgruntled growl.

"I know we should be with her, but we're too slow and too loud," Judd said in a low voice. "We need to trust our mate."

His bear settled slightly, and Judd watched as Tori took another peek at Andrew and his friends. They were either staring at the fire or at each other, and Judd's heart lurched when Tori took off toward the barn door.

"Holy fuck," he breathed as he watched her sprint toward the door. "She's so fucking fast."

She was at the door in less than four seconds, pulling it open just a crack and slipping inside before shutting it behind her.

Judd paced, keeping his gaze trained on the door. A minute went by, then two, and then five. "C'mon, Tori-girl. Where the fuck are you? Get your gorgeous ass out of the barn and... oh shit."

He watched, his heart beating frantically as Andrew and a pretty blonde girl broke off from the group at the bonfire and headed toward the barn. Judd briefly considered changing to his bear form and running out into the yard as a distraction, but Andrew was already pulling open the door and ushering the girl inside.

"Fuuuuck," Judd said. He waited another five agonizing minutes before stripping off his shirt. He had to do something. He couldn't stand here with his thumb up his ass while Tori was trapped in the barn. He'd shift to his bear form and charge the bonfire. The screams of the others would bring Andrew and his girlfriend out of the barn and give Tori time to get out with the device. He'd just have to hope that Andrew's mother didn't have a shotgun in the damn house.

He unbuttoned his jeans and hooked his hands in the waistband. He paused when the light gray rabbit hopped up to the tree and stared at him, its nose twitching rapidly.

"Tori?" he said. "Uh, is that you?"

With a soft pop, the rabbit transformed into the gloriously

naked Tori. She studied his bare chest and his unbuttoned pants. "Whatcha' doin', big guy?"

"What do you mean what I am doing? I was about to create a distraction so you could get out of the barn."

She grabbed his shirt from where he'd dropped it and put it on. "You're sweet."

"Where's the device?" he asked.

She made a face. "I didn't get it. It took me a few minutes to remember which fucking stall had the loose boards."

"Shit. Did you see it? Is it still there?"

She nodded as he grabbed his jacket and shrugged into it. "It's still there. I had my fucking hand on it when Andrew and his girlfriend entered the barn. I had to drop my clothes under the floorboards with the device and shift to my bunny form. The little horndogs started making out right in front of the fucking stall."

"Did they see you in your bunny form?" he asked.

"No. They were too busy competing to touch the other's tonsils first to notice me." She grimaced. "I probably could have walked out of there in my human form with the device."

"So, we wait again," Judd said.

She shook her head. "Andrew told Vanessa that his mom was asleep so they could party all night. They were about to break out the weed and the beer and move the party into the barn."

"Fucking teenagers," Judd said.

"Yeah. There's no point in us freezing our asses off for the rest of the night. We'll come back tomorrow night and grab it," Tori said.

Disappointed but worried that Tori's lips were already turning blue, Judd scooped her up. "C'mon, let's get you to the car."

"I can walk," she said as her teeth chattered and her body shook.

"In your bare feet in the snow? No," he said, "absolutely not."

She kissed his cheek. "Thank you, my sweet bear."

CHAPTER 20

"They're here," Judd said.

Anxiety weaving its way through her stomach, Tori stood up from the bed as Judd opened the motel door.

It was early afternoon, and Hudson had texted Judd about half an hour ago to ask if he, Mal, Bishop, and Kat could drop by.

She watched as Hudson ducked into the room, followed by Mal, Kat, and then Bishop, who was also forced to duck through the doorway. The three bear shifters clustered together near the desk, and their previously big enough motel room seemed to shrink to dollhouse size. Bishop was a grizzly shifter and nearly as big as Hudson, and Judd was one of the biggest black bear shifters she'd ever met. She swallowed down the claustrophobia creeping in.

"Hello, Tori," Mal said.

"Hi, Mal." She smiled at the wolf shifter before saying hello to Kat and Bishop.

Mal leaned against the wall, studying her thoughtfully. "Tell me about the building and the laboratory."

She took a quick swig of water. "The building itself is three floors…."

———

"Okay, so you said there's twenty-four hour security in the building lobby," Mal said.

"There used to be," Tori said. "But I doubt that's changed, so I think we're safe to assume there still is."

Mal turned to Kat. "If we get Clay into the lobby, is that enough of a hum for him to get to the laboratory below the building?"

The jaguar shifter shook her head. "I can confirm with him, but I don't think it works that way. I think he needs to see the actual lab to hear its hum."

"What do you mean by hum?" Tori asked.

Kat stared blankly at her for a few seconds. "Sorry, you have no idea how weird it is to hear you talk in that voice."

"Word," Bishop said.

"I'm not sure if this is a compliment, but you did the dumb bunny routine well," Kat said.

Tori grinned a little. "Thanks." In her old life, she and Kat would have been friends. She was sure of it. The jaguar was smart, tough, and precisely the kind of woman Tori would want to spend time with.

"Clay occasionally works with us and has a… special ability," Kat said. "One that we might be able to use to get some serum from the lab."

"You can tell them," Bishop said. "I know Judd won't say a word, and considering Tori has been living a double life for how many years, pretty sure she won't say anything either."

Kat studied both of them. "I'll trust that you'll keep this to yourself. But know that if you ever consider telling someone, Clay is a very dangerous man, and it's doubtful that any of us in this room will be able to stop him from killing you to protect his secret."

"He sounds like a real great guy," Judd said.

"He is a good man, but he won't hesitate to protect himself or the people he loves from anyone who tries to use his abilities for their gain," Kat said. "Clay's a teleport."

"Holy shit," Judd said. "I thought they were a fucking myth."

"So does everyone," Bishop said.

"I heard a rumour that there was one in Tanzania," Tori said. "The military took him, and no one's seen him since."

"They probably dissected him and put all the pieces that were left into tiny jars," Hudson said moodily.

"Clay has to see a place to teleport into it," Kat said. "It works best if he sees it himself, but he can work off a video if necessary."

Mal rubbed at the scruff on his jaw. "What if we hacked the cameras in the lab? Clay could watch the security feed of the lab cameras, and that might be enough."

"Francis uses a high-tech computer system for security," Tori said. "It's nearly impossible to crack."

Bishop shrugged. "We have Kat."

Pink flushed Kat's cheeks, but she gave Bishop a pleased look.

"You're a computer hacker?" Tori asked.

"I dabble," Kat said.

Mal rolled his eyes. "You more than dabble, Kat."

"You're willing to risk your entire firm if you get caught?" Tori said. "This is some highly illegal shit we're about to do."

Mal stared steadily at her. "Everyone in this room wants children. This Francis guy needs to be stopped, and we need proof. Once we have the serum, and the device, we have a friend on the police force you can speak with. You tell him what Francis is planning and that you took the serum and device to stop him."

"So she can be arrested for theft?" Judd said with a tinge of anger.

"Bren won't arrest her," Bishop said. "Especially when he finds out what Francis is trying to do."

"If he even believes us," Tori said. "It's not like I know how the machine works and can prove to him what it does."

"Bren will believe you," Bishop said. "Trust me. He's the mate of one of my best friends, and he's helped us before with shit that wasn't exactly on the up and up."

"Do you have the device?" Hudson asked Judd.

He shook his head. "We tried to get it last night but were thwarted by a group of horny teenagers. We'll go back tonight and get it."

"Then we have a plan," Mal said. "We'll work on getting a serum sample while you two work with the witch to break the protection spell on the device. Do you want me to send a couple of people with you to grab the device?"

Tori shook her head. "Thanks, but no. It's a family of squirrel shifters, and you know how well they can smell. I don't want the mom spooked if she starts smelling a bunch of different animals around the property. Judd and I can handle this on our own."

"Okay." Mal headed toward the door, and as the others followed, Tori glanced at Judd before stepping forward.

"Before you leave, I want to say thank you for helping me."

Judd's hand slipped into hers, and she held it tightly, grateful for the support. "It means a lot that you all have my back even though you don't really know me."

Mal studied her before his gaze slipped to Judd for a second. "Judd's our friend and a good man. A good man who saved my brother's life once and whom I have a great deal of respect for. Even if Francis weren't about to fuck the entire world, we would be more than happy to help. You're Judd's mate, and he's asked us to help you. That's all the reason we need."

They filed out of the hotel room. Hudson left last, but not before he showed Judd a few pics of Linda on his phone. Tori could smell Judd's relief from across the room when Hudson showed him a picture of Linda cuddled up with Rosalie on the couch, and her mate's happiness made her bunny nearly delirious with glee.

Not your mate.

She nodded to Hudson as he ducked out of the hotel room with a final goodbye and a promise to give Linda a kiss from Judd. Judd locked the door before leaning against it. His cheeks that cute shade of pink again, he said, "Sorry about the mate thing. I should have corrected Mal, but I…."

"No, it's fine," she said. "We smell like each other, so it's not like they don't know we're having sex. Plus, you're risking your life for me. It's not surprising that he thinks I'm your mate."

She swallowed hard, feeling awkward and dumb and desperately holding back her urge to tell Judd she wanted to be his mate for real. She could smell his discomfort, and holy fuck, she'd rather be in the middle of a gunfight than in this horrifyingly awkward situation.

She forced a smile to her face, grabbing her phone and waving it at him. "Hey, you hungry? We should probably order something to eat. What do you feel like? Italian, maybe? Or something simple like pizza or burgers or -"

"Tori," Judd said. "I want more."

She thought about saying something pithy about his insatiable appetite for food, but the words wouldn't come. Not when Judd stared at her with those gorgeous dark eyes that told her exactly what he meant.

"I want to be more than just your fuck buddy. I want us to date," Judd said.

His willingness to put it all out there despite what they'd both said earlier sent warmth rushing over her. Her bear was brave and kind, and perfect. She would have to be a damn fool to reject him, and while she might have been a lot of things, a damn fool wasn't one of them.

"I want to date you, too," she said.

His growl of happiness was way too cute, as was the way he immediately stormed over and picked her up, kissing her until she was breathless.

"Thank fucking Christ," he said.

She smoothed her hands through his thick, dark hair. "Judd, have you thought about this, though? I'm not the Tori you've known for the last few years. I can't go back to the dumb bunny routine, and I -"

"I don't want the dumb bunny routine," Judd said. "I want you for exactly who you are - a terrifying assassin who could probably kill me with her bare hands."

She laughed hard. "I'm not an assassin, you dork."

"You're not *not* an assassin," he said with that grin she fucking loved.

She stroked his hair again and wrapped her legs around his waist, loving how hard he got just from that simple motion. "We have a decision to make."

"What's that?" he asked, one hand caressing her ass.

"Do we want to eat, or do we want to fuck?"

"Why not both?" he said.

Her smile widened. "Both, it is."

CHAPTER 21

"You ready to go?" Judd asked.

Tori nodded. "It might be better if I go alone. Less chance of us being caught if it's just me."

"You're not going alone," Judd said.

Tori gave him an exasperated look. "I say this in the nicest way possible, but you're not known for stealth or speed. If I go by myself, then -"

"No," Judd said. "We're a team, remember? We do this together."

He had a feeling that Tori would keep arguing, but his phone buzzing saved him. He pulled it out of his pocket and read the screen. "Shit."

"What's wrong?"

"Fenton says someone is watching our room." Judd called the cheetah shifter, putting the call on speaker when Fenton answered. "Hey, Fenton, you're sure?"

"Yes," Fenton said. "Human male in a beige Honda parked two spots in front of me. Garrett was covering the night shift. I gave him a description of the guy and the car, and Garrett said he drove by the motel a few times around two this morning but didn't stick around. He showed up again at eight this morning, parked his ass on the street, and hasn't left since."

"Has he made you, do you think?" Judd asked.

"I don't think so," Fenton said. "He's pretty focused on your room. Plus, he's a human. Half the time, they don't notice fucking shit when it comes to shifters. If this Francis guy is a shifter, why did he send a human to keep an eye on you?"

"Because he thinks humans are disposable," Tori said. "And he knows what I'll do to the human if I discover him following me."

Judd glanced at his watch. "We need to get to the farm and grab the device, but if this asshole follows us and tells Francis, we're fucked."

"I'll stop the guy from following you," Fenton said. "Just give me the heads up when you're leaving."

"We're leaving in two minutes," Tori said.

"I'll be ready," Fenton said and ended the call.

"How did he find us?" Judd paced the room, his bear growling softly.

Tori caught his hand, pulling him to a stop. "Honestly, it doesn't matter how he found us. What matters is destroying the machine before Francis can take it from us. We have to go, my bear. The quicker we get the machine to Elora, the better."

"Right." Judd squeezed Tori's hand. "Ready?"

She nodded, and they stepped outside into the cold night air and walked briskly toward Judd's SUV. The Honda was parked under a street lamp, and Judd glanced casually at it as he unlocked the car. The human was a shadowy lump in the driver's side, and Judd paused when Tori said, "I'll drive."

He handed the keys to her without protest and climbed

into the passenger side as Tori slid behind the wheel and started the vehicle.

"Did you recognize the guy?" Judd asked.

"I couldn't make out his features," Tori said. "You know bunnies see about as well as humans in the dark."

"Why did you want to drive?"

"Because if the cheetah shifter doesn't stop him from following us, we need to lose him before we go to the farm. I'm pretty sure you don't have experience in ditching a tail."

Judd grinned despite his anxiety. "You'd be correct."

She wiggled her nose at him, giving him a cute grin. "That's okay. I still think you're hot."

"Thanks." He reached across and squeezed her thigh lightly as she turned out of the parking lot and drove down the street. They passed Fenton's car, and then the human's car and Judd watched in the rearview mirror as the Honda's headlights flicked on.

"Here he comes," he said.

"If Fenton isn't successful, I'll -"

Judd grinned at the metallic-sounding crunch and squealing brakes. "Holy fuck, Fenton just hit the guy's car as he pulled out onto the street."

A red light at the end of the street forced Tori to stop. Judd twisted in his seat, watching under the glow of the street lamps as Fenton climbed out of his car. He had smashed into the Honda's driver's side, caving in the rear wheel arch panel and popping the tire. It had already deflated, and the human kicked at the tire before gesturing angrily at Fenton. The cheetah shifter rubbed his neck and back before glaring at the human.

"C'mon," Tori muttered under her breath as she stared at the light.

"Trust me, the guy's not going anywhere," Judd said.

"Fenton completely took out his back tire. Mal might kill him when he sees the damage to the car."

The light changed, and Tori stepped on the gas and took the next left. Judd squeezed her thigh lightly as she checked the rearview mirror and took a right down a side street. "He's not following us, Tori-girl."

"I know," she said. "But it doesn't hurt to take a few extra turns just to make sure there isn't anyone else following us before we head out to the farm." She glanced at him. "Trust me on this, Judd."

He nodded and sat back in his seat. He could smell Tori's worry and anxiety and rubbed her thigh gently. "This will work, Tori. We'll destroy the machine, and you'll finally get your life back."

Tori nodded, but the scent of her anxiety didn't lessen. His bear growled softly. He didn't like it when their mate was upset.

Mate? She's not your mate. She agreed to date, but that doesn't make her your mate, Judd. Don't go thinking it does. Tori's been alone a long time, and it'll take more than great sex to break down her walls and earn her trust.

He knew that, but it wasn't like he could stop his bear from thinking of Tori as his mate. Hell, the damn thing was in love with her and had been for a long time.

He's not the only one in love with her.

He continued to stroke Tori's thigh, staring blankly out the window. Telling Tori he was in love with her would only scare her away. He just needed to be patient and hope that, with time, she would see him as her mate.

———

"FUCK ME, I HATE THAT KID," JUDD MUTTERED.

Tori made herself smile, even though she could have cheerfully strangled the teen squirrel shifter herself. "He'll go in the house soon."

They watched from the tree line as Andrew took another puff of his joint before blowing smoke rings. He wore earbuds, and his head bopped along to the beat only he could hear. The smell of marijuana was thick in the air, and Judd's bear grumbled a complaint.

"Why's he even bothering to hide behind the barn?" Judd said in a low voice. "His mother will know the minute he walks back into the house. That shit reeks like he got it at a fucking dollar store."

"It blocks the wind," Tori said. The Solum Winds were blowing hard tonight, kicking up a combination of snow and grit. She slid her arms around Judd's waist, and not just because she and her bunny loved touching Judd. They'd been standing outside waiting for Andrew to go inside for the last half hour, and, thanks to the howling winds, she was freezing her ass off. Judd put his arms around her, and she reveled in his heat. "He'll go inside soon. If he doesn't, I'll kill him."

Judd stiffened against her, and she grinned at him. "Relax, big guy. That's just a little assassin humour."

"So, you finally admit you're an assassin," he said with a soft chuckle. "What will you do once this is all over?"

"What do you mean?" she asked.

"Will you keep working at Bud's?"

"No," she said. "I hate being a waitress."

"That's fair," he said.

She stared up at him, his face barely visible in the darkness. "I want to reconnect with my family. Thanks to Francis, I've barely spoken to them for years, and even though I'm not particularly close with my mom, I know it hurts her that I'm always making excuses for not seeing her or my siblings."

"I'm surprised you haven't run into one of them here in the city," Judd said.

"Only my mom and six of my siblings still live here. The rest of them are living all over the world. But they all return to visit Mom regularly. I'm the only one who hasn't, and most of my siblings have completely stopped talking to me. They're pissed that I'm so distant with them, and I can't blame them."

"It's not your fault," Judd said.

She wished like hell she could believe that. "As I said before, sometimes I go to Mom's house and watch her garden, but I haven't spoken to her in person or hugged her since the night I took the device from Francis."

He rubbed her back and kissed her forehead. "That will change soon, I promise."

She wanted to believe him, hoped he was right, but it'd been a long time since her life had been anything more than running and hiding and always looking over her shoulder. Even now, there were so many doubts crowding in. Nothing would change if Elora couldn't break the spell and Mal and the others couldn't get a serum sample. She'd have to leave again, and this time, she wouldn't just be leaving a job and an apartment. She'd be leaving Judd. Her mate.

Tell him we love him, her bunny pleaded. *Please.*

She couldn't. Not when the threat of having to leave him was still very real. What good would it do to confess her love for him when she might have to leave him?

Judd sniffed the air, and she peered around him into the dark woods. "Do you smell something?"

"Hard to tell, thanks to the smell of that fucking weed," he said. "I smell a few animals, a moose, a bear, and a deer, maybe. But that doesn't mean they're shifters."

"Francis has been using humans," Tori said. "I haven't smelled any humans, have you?"

"No," he said. "But what are the odds he might send someone here to look for you?"

"It could happen," she admitted. "But if he had, wouldn't they have tried to take us last night?"

"Yeah," Judd said. "Still, the sooner we get that machine and get the fuck out of here, the better."

"Agreed," Tori said. "Maybe we could -"

"Thank fucking Christ," Judd said when Andrew stubbed out the joint against the side of the barn before heading toward the farmhouse. They waited another five minutes, watching the quiet farmhouse for any signs of the squirrel shifters before Tori squeezed Judd's hand.

"Let's go."

He nodded, and they crept along the tree line until they were beside the barn. "Ready?" Tori breathed.

"Yes," he said.

Tori let go of his hand and sprinted for the barn doors. Judd was surprisingly quick for his size, but she still had to temper her speed so he could keep up. She opened the left door enough for them to squeeze through, then closed it quietly.

"Fuck," Judd pounded at his chest with one hand, "I gotta add more cardio to my workout routine."

"You did well, my bear," she said. "Come on. The machine is in the third stall."

They walked down the wide and dusty aisle to the third stall. She peered inside. "Well, fuck."

"What's wrong?" Judd looked into the stall. "What the fuck are those?"

"Old wagon wheels," Tori said. "They weren't in here last night."

"Christ, how many are here?" Judd asked.

"At least a dozen," Tori said as she studied the wooden wheels piled in the stall.

"What the fuck are they using them for?"

"No idea, but we'll have to move them to get to the loose floorboards."

"Fucking hell," Judd said, but he was already removing his jacket. Working together and trying to be quiet, they moved the wheels one by one into the aisle.

"Thank God I didn't convince you to stay at the motel," Tori puffed as they lugged, or rather Judd lugged, another wheel out of the stall. "I could never have moved these on my own."

Judd grunted as he lifted a smaller wheel over his head and carried it into the aisle. They worked quickly, but another twenty minutes had passed before they could get to the floorboards.

Tori pried up the loose boards and hopped down under the floor. She grabbed the device and handed it to Judd before boosting herself out.

"What about your clothes from last night?" Judd asked as she carefully notched the floorboards back into place.

"I don't need them," she said.

He stared at the grey box in his hands, turning it over a few times before studying the row of buttons on the side. "This is it, huh?"

"That's it."

"I thought it would be bigger."

She just shrugged and took it from him. "C'mon, let's get out of here."

"What about the wheels?" Judd said. "Shouldn't we put them back?"

"Leave them," she said. "Let that pot-smoking teenager

move them all back. He's young and doesn't have a bad back."

Judd snorted soft laughter before following her down the aisle toward the doors. "Isn't that the fucking truth."

She cracked the door and listened carefully before glancing at the farmhouse and driveway. "I don't hear or see anything, do you?"

Judd shook his head. "No, let's get the fuck out of here."

She took his hand, and they stepped out of the barn. Her muscles bunched in preparation for her sprint back to the safety of the trees, but before they'd taken a single step, the headlights of the squirrel shifter's SUV turned on, bathing them in bright light.

She squinted, dropping Judd's hand to hold her hand up and block the light as Judd's bear made a low, deep growl. A grizzly shifter stepped out from behind the SUV as the farmhouse door opened, and Andrew, his mother, and his sister, Mari, stumbled out.

Tori's stomach dropped when Francis stepped out behind them. A black bear shifter, jaguar shifter, and the fox shifter from the bar followed Francis, and she took Judd's hand, squeezing it hard as he made another deep growl.

"Be calm, my bear," she said.

The bear shifter herded the squirrel shifter family into the light from the headlights. They huddled together, both kids clinging to their mother as Francis stepped into the light.

"Hello, Astoria."

Her stomach in knots, she swallowed hard and said, "Hello, Francis."

CHAPTER 22

J udd's bear was about to lose his fucking shit. He wanted Judd to shift. He wanted to tear apart the shifters who threatened his mate. Judd kept control by the barest of threads. Tori's hand in his was the only thing keeping him tethered to his human side.

"It's been a long time, Astoria." Francis smiled at her. "You look good."

"I see you're still wearing those fucking cowboy boots," Tori said. "They look even more ridiculous than I remember."

Francis's smile widened. "God, I've missed you."

"How did you find me?" Tori asked.

"I never thought you'd hide the device on Tamatha and Dan's farm," Francis said. "Didn't think you were that stupid, but I guess I'm the one who's a fool. You played the 'this is the last place he'd expect me to put it, so I'll put it here' game, and I fell for it. One of my more embarrassing moments, if I'm being truthful. But, with time running out and you being here in the city, I asked my fox friend to watch the farm. Just in case."

Francis smiled at the fox shifter. "It was a desperate move on my part, but one that paid off."

He turned back to Tori. "Once the fox told me that you and your," he stared at Judd with barely concealed disgust, "boyfriend were here, I knew in my very soul that the device was here. But I made myself wait. I couldn't afford to make any mistakes, not when time was so limited. In fact, I thought we would run out of time and everything I'd worked for would be in vain. But all I needed was to see you with the device in hand. So, we followed you back to your motel, but I was very clever, Astoria. I've learned my lesson with you. I kept the fox here in case the human I sent to watch you at your motel fucked up."

Francis shook his head. "Which he did because he's a human, and they're fucking useless."

He took a deep breath. "When the fox told me you were back, I immediately gathered my friends and headed here. I knew you would show me where my device was this time, Astoria."

He smiled benignly at her. "And I was right."

Tori's grip on his hand tightened, and his bear made a rumbling growl that had the black bear and grizzly bear shifters bearing their fangs at him.

"Why are you suddenly using shifters?" Tori asked.

"Humans are weak," Francis said, "but they have their uses. But when I need shit done, I use shifters. You know that."

When Tori didn't reply, Francis said, "Why did you come back here? Why did you crawl out of whatever dark hole you'd buried yourself in and return to me?"

"Don't flatter yourself. It had nothing to do with you," Tori said.

"I don't believe that," Francis said softly. "You missed your father."

"You are not my father," Tori said. "You're a fucking monster."

"I'm trying to save the world, and you call me a monster. I don't know where I went wrong with you, Astoria. You wanted to change the world as well, remember?"

"Until I stopped drinking the Kool-Aid," Tori said.

"No, until you got cold feet," Francis snapped.

"This isn't a case of cold fucking feet," Tori said. "You're insane, and I won't let you take the machine."

"Yes, you will. Or I'll kill your boyfriend and the squirrel shifters." Francis stroked the little girl's hair, making her chitter anxiously and cling harder to her mother. "Do you want to be responsible for the death of this pretty little child, Astoria?"

Tori's face paled, and Judd squeezed her hand before staring at Francis. "You're not taking the device."

"No one's talking to you, bear shifter," Francis said dismissively. He stared at Tori before stroking Mari's hair again. "You have two choices, Astoria. You can hand over the device, and no one dies today. Or, you can take the device and run straight into those woods. You're faster than any of us, and we'll never catch you. But, in doing so, you will kill the man you love and three innocents."

Tori stared up at Judd, and he knew what she would do before she squeezed his hand and said, "I'm sorry."

She dropped his hand and walked toward Francis. He stayed where he was, despite how his bear roared at him to protect their mate. Sweat broke out on his body, and he concentrated fiercely on holding his bear back as Tori handed the device to Francis.

He smiled at her. "Thank you, Astoria. Let's go."

He took her wrist, and Judd let loose with a roar of anger that echoed through the forest. He started toward them, fur sprouting across his face and fangs lengthening. He stopped abruptly when the jaguar shifter wrapped one hand around Tori's throat and squeezed.

"If you shift, he'll kill her," Francis said.

His bear retreated immediately, the sounds of Tori choking sending horror rocketing through Judd and his bear. Francis nodded, and the jaguar shifter released Tori. Coughing and gagging, she staggered back toward Judd. He wrapped his arm around her waist, pulling her in tight against his body.

"I'm okay, big guy," she gasped before massaging her throat.

Francis studied the device, the glow of madness and delight radiating from his gaze. "Finally."

"You have what you wanted. Get the fuck out of here," Judd growled.

Francis stared at him and then at Tori, his gaze dropping to Judd's arm around her waist. "Astoria, it's time to go."

Judd pulled her even closer as his bear snarled with anger. "Not fucking happening."

Francis pointed to Mari, and the grizzly shifter picked her up, grinning at her with his sharp fangs as he dangled her in front of him. Mari's mother rushed toward them, and Francis punched her hard in the stomach. She dropped to her knees, coughing and sucking in air as Andrew cried out and crouched beside her.

"Come with me, Astoria, and your boyfriend and the innocents live. Choose to stay, and you'll watch them die, starting with the little girl."

Judd could smell Tori's fear and sorrow, and he squeezed her hip. "Tori, baby, you can't."

She reached up and cupped his face, stroking his beard that was rapidly turning to fur. "Shh, my bear. Do not shift. It'll be all right."

"He'll kill you," Judd said. "If you go with him, he'll kill you."

"I don't think so," she said. "But if I don't, he'll definitely kill you."

"Baby, I can't let you go," Judd said.

She stood on her tiptoes and kissed him. "You have to."

She kissed him again before hugging him hard. She pressed her mouth to his ear. "I love you, my mate."

She pushed away and crossed the short distance to stand beside Francis before Judd could say anything.

Francis smiled smugly at Judd, making him want to crack the antelope shifter in half. He clenched his hands into fists as the wind howled its mournful cry. Tori's long hair was in a ponytail, and Francis stroked her hair with his free hand. Still smiling that smug fucking grin, Francis glanced at the fox shifter. "Get the car."

The shifter jogged down the driveway, disappearing into the darkness.

"Here's what's going to happen," Francis said. "The bear shifters will stay here with your boyfriend and this lovely family while you come with me, and we finish what we started so many years ago. If you're a good little bunny, they live. If you're not, they die. Simple, is it not, Astoria?"

"When this is over, then what?" she asked.

"We let everyone go," Francis said. "You can live the rest of your life with your new love. There may even be a chance that your mate is one of the lucky ones and isn't affected. You could push out your 2.3 children, have a house in suburbia with a white picket fence, and live your perfect life."

"You can't trust him. He'll kill us anyway," Judd said.

"I'm not the murderer," Francis stroked Tori's hair again, "she is."

Judd hated how Tori's face paled, how the sick look of shame crossed her face. He dug his nails into his palms, relishing the pain when they pierced through his skin and blood dripped from his fists.

"This will all be over by tomorrow afternoon," Francis said. "You'll have your life back, Astoria, and I'll start a new one as the saviour of the world."

"You're fucking insane," Judd said.

Francis laughed. "No, I'm the most brilliant man you'll ever meet, bear shifter."

"Promise me you won't hurt them." Tori stepped away from Francis, staring steadily at him.

"I promise," Francis said.

"He's lying," Judd said.

"I'm a bastard, but I'm not a liar," Francis said. "Astoria knows that."

Tori eyed the other shifters, and, desperation in his voice, Judd said, "We can end this right here together, baby."

She stared at the two bear shifters before studying him, and Judd's bear whimpered at the look of resignation on his mate's face. She was tough and strong, but she was still only a bunny. She could give the grizzly or the bear shifter a run for their money, but she wouldn't defeat them, and she didn't believe he could, either. Not after he'd told her he almost died fighting two bear shifters.

She's right. You won't defeat them. So use your fucking brains and keep calm, and maybe you and your mate will survive.

He wanted so badly to believe his inner voice, but his worry for his mate, his fear he would never see her again, nearly obliterated his ability to think straight.

"It'll be okay, my mate." Tori's soft voice pulled him back from the edge again. "Stay calm. We'll be together again."

He studied her face as the wind howled and shrieked. She returned his stare and even managed to give him a small smile as a black sedan pulled into the driveway. The jaguar shifter opened the back door as Francis took Tori's hand and led her toward the car. "Time to go, Astoria."

"Tori!" Judd had to shout to be heard over the wind.

She looked over her shoulder at him, her face ghostly pale in the dim light.

"I love you, my mate," Judd said.

His bear roared in panic and anger when Francis shoved Tori into the backseat of the car before she could reply and climbed in behind her. The jaguar slid into the front seat, and the car drove away. Judd stared at the two bear shifters, a calmness settling over him.

He had no doubt they would kill him, but he wouldn't make it easy on them.

CHAPTER 23

The black bear and grizzly shifter moved to flank the squirrel family. The grizzly shifter had long black hair that blew around his face as he grunted at Judd. "Get over here with the squirrels."

"You're going to kill us now, aren't you?" Judd said as he walked slowly toward them.

The grizzly shifter grinned. "Not now, but once the boss releases the serum in the morning, he'll call me, and it's lights out for you and the squirrels. Don't worry, though. We'll make it quick and painless. Mostly."

"Guess your boss is a liar after all, huh?" Judd said.

The grizzly shrugged before glancing at the squirrels. "They're only dying because of you, Judd. The boss wants the little bitch bunny back at his side, and he knows it won't happen with you around. So, you gotta fucking go, and these poor folks right here? They're just in the wrong place at the wrong time. No hard feelings, though, yeah? It's just business."

"Killing innocent shifters is just business?" Judd said.

Andrew and Mari's mother pulled away from her children and chittered to them.

They chittered back, their eyes wide and fearful as Andrew put his arms around his sister.

"Shut the fuck up," the black bear shifter snarled before shoving the mother in the back, nearly pitching her onto her knees. He was broad and beefy looking with olive-coloured skin and beady dark eyes that glittered in the light. "God, I hate the sound of your chittering. Use your words when you're in your human form, you stupid bitch."

She ignored him and chittered to her children again. Judd didn't understand squirrel, but whatever she said had Andrew gazing at the trees.

"I said, shut the fuck up before I smash your teeth in." The black bear shifter made a squawk of surprise when he reached for the squirrel shifter, and her clothes collapsed. He stared dumbly at the pile of clothing before glancing at the grizzly shifter. "Where the fuck did she go?"

Andrew and Mari's clothes collapsed, and the dark grey squirrel zipped out from beneath the mother's clothing pile. Judd watched in shock as she scampered up the man's body and sank her teeth into his throat with a high-pitched squeal.

The black bear shifter bellowed in pain and tore her off him before hurling her to the ground. She landed on the pile of clothing and bounced off it, her small body flying through the air before landing on her feet with a jarring thud. She chittered to her children, and they squirmed out from their clothing in their squirrel forms, and the three of them took off for the trees.

"Fuck!" The grizzly shifter snarled. He took a few steps toward the trees before turning around to face the bear shifter. "Go get those fucking squirrels while I ... oh fuck me."

"What?" The black bear shifter gave him a dazed look. "What's wrong?"

Judd stared at the blood spurting out from the black bear's neck at an alarming rate. The squirrel shifter had gone straight for the jugular, and Judd's bear growled in delight at the blood spraying out of the torn and bitten skin.

"She fucked you up, man. She really fucked you up," the grizzly shifter said.

"I don't feel so good," the black bear shifter slurred before dropping to his knees. He touched his throat, staring blankly at the red that coated his fingers. "Is that… blood?"

He collapsed on his face, and Judd called for his bear with a low growl.

His bear surged forward, and Judd shifted with a soft pop before rushing the grizzly shifter. The grizzly shifted immediately and charged forward.

Judd's bear snarled when the grizzly stood on his hind legs and swiped at him. Judd ducked and rammed his shoulder into the grizzly's midsection, knocking him off balance. He roared in pain when the grizzly raked its claws down his back, tearing through his thick fur. He ignored the hot blood soaking into his fur and attacked again, swiping one big paw across the grizzly's face.

The grizzly screamed in pain, and Judd roared with satisfaction when he felt the grizzly's eye puncture beneath his claw. The grizzly sank his teeth into Judd's shoulder, and the searing pain forced him to his knees.

The grizzly snarled triumphantly and released Judd's shoulder before raising his paw to deliver the death blow. Judd rolled away, the grizzly's razor-sharp claws narrowly missing his throat. He jumped to his feet and rushed forward, dragging his right paw across the grizzly's stomach.

The grizzly squealed and staggered back, watching in

disbelief as his fur and skin parted, and his intestines slithered out to land in a wet pile on the ground. He shifted to his human form and slowly sank to his knees before trying to gather up the slippery ropes of his intestines.

"That hurt, man," he whined as he picked up a long loop of intestine. "That really fucking…."

He pitched over on his side, the light in his eyes fading as the loops of intestines slipped from his hands back onto the ground.

Judd's bear roared his victory and then grumbled when Judd made a push for control. He pushed again, and his bear retreated. Judd turned to stare at the dark grey squirrel sniffing at the dead black bear. She shifted to her human form and kicked the bear with a low grunt. "Asshole."

She glanced at Judd. "You're bleeding."

He touched his back. "It'll heal."

"Yeah, but you need to stop the bleeding first. I don't need three dead bear shifters in my driveway."

Andrew and Mari joined them as their mother yanked on her jeans and shirt. "You guys okay?"

Andrew changed to his human form. "That was so fucking badass, Mom. You killed a bear shifter."

"Yeah, well, he shouldn't have threatened my kids," she said. She petted Mari's head. "It's okay, my love. You can shift to your human form."

Mari shifted, and her mother helped her into her clothes as Andrew pulled on his jeans. "Andrew, go into the house and get as many spare towels from the upstairs closet as you can carry. Mari, go help him."

"Are you okay, Mama?" Mari asked.

"I'm fine, my love. I need you to be brave for a little longer, all right?

"Okay," she said.

"Go with your brother, quickly."

The two children ran into the house, and Judd crouched beside his ruined clothing. He wrapped what was left of his shirt around his waist like a makeshift skirt before he found his cell phone and straightened. He winced painfully as his back burned and blood soaked into the shirt around his waist.

"Come into the house, bear shifter," the mother said.

"It's Judd," he said.

"Alice," she said.

"I have to go," Judd said. "I need to find my mate."

"You'll bleed to death first if you don't let me help you," she said.

Alice was right. He was healing, but blood loss would kill him before he could fully heal if he didn't apply some fucking pressure to the wounds.

"You can't call the cops," he said. "Not until I leave."

She studied him as they walked slowly toward the house. "I don't suppose you're gonna tell me what the fuck is going on, huh?"

"It's a long story," Judd said.

"It always is," Alice said as she opened the door. "Come on, let's get the bleeding stopped."

TORI PACED THE SMALL WINDOWLESS ROOM. FRANCIS HAD taken her phone, and she had no idea what time it was, but she guessed early morning. The room had a twin bed and nothing else, but she hadn't slept. Instead, she'd alternated between sitting on the bed and pacing, her stomach in knots and her bunny pissed off.

"Give it a rest, for fuck's sake," she muttered when her

bunny demanded again for her to kill Francis. "Killing Francis means killing our mate. Use your head."

Her bunny's immediate panic at the thought of their mate dying made Tori feel guilty for being such a bitch.

It's all right, my sweet. Our mate is safe as long as we do what Francis wants.

Her bunny settled a little, and Tori resumed pacing. She might have convinced her bunny, but convincing herself wasn't quite as easy. Francis would kill Judd. She was sure of it. But she had no fucking clue how to save him, and it filled her with barely containable terror.

The lock clicked, and the door opened. Francis stepped into the room and smiled at her. "How did you sleep, Astoria?"

"Unless you want me to piss on the floor, I need a bathroom," Tori said.

Francis laughed. "I really have missed you. I'll take you to the bathroom, and then we'll have breakfast together. It's a big day for us."

Ten minutes later, she sat in a small kitchen, watching the sun rise through the window over the sink as Francis made them spinach omelets. The jaguar shifter from last night – he had thick blond hair and a surly expression - stood near the doorway, watching Tori closely.

"Astoria, this is Jaden, my head of security." Francis pulled the eggs and spinach out of the fridge.

"Are you afraid of me, Francis?" Tori asked.

Francis grinned. "Of course I am. I'm no fool, Astoria. Now, I know you're fast, but Jaden is faster, so keep your hands to yourself. Unless you want your bear boyfriend to die."

He set the pan on the stove. "I'm disappointed in your

choice of mate, Astoria. The shifter is barely above a Neanderthal."

"Like I give a fuck what you think of Judd," Tori said.

"There was a time when my opinion mattered to you very much," Francis said.

"Because I was an idiot," Tori said. "How did you find me here?"

"Your zebra friend Rick, as a matter of fact. He still works for me. He saw you in the grocery store." Francis's laugh was close to a cackle. "I still don't understand why you came back to Ashdale. You couldn't possibly think that changing your hair colour and growing it out would be enough to keep you safe. Rick recognized you right away. Honestly, I'm surprised he didn't attack you right there among the produce. You did shoot him after all. Of course, you know how zebra shifters are… they act tough, but once you show them who's alpha, they get on their knees pretty quick. Anyway, he followed my little missing bunny back to her little bunny burrow, and the very next morning, he was in my office telling me just how to find you. And now here we are. Together again."

"Hur-fucking-rah," Tori said.

"Do you remember when we went on vacation together to that wretched little town in Montana?" Francis cracked the eggs in a bowl and added a healthy dollop of cream before whipping them with a fork.

Tori didn't reply, and Francis glanced at her. "We ordered spinach omelets at that diner with the mostly burnt-out neon sign. They'd never even heard of spinach. Do you remember?"

He added some seasoning and the spinach and poured the egg mixture into the hot pan. "We had a lot of good times together, Astoria."

"Until you lost your fucking mind," she said.

He sighed and grabbed a spatula from the drawer. "Out of everyone, I truly believed that you would be the one to understand why this needs to be done. The fact that you didn't and still don't, breaks my heart."

"Liar," she said. "If you'd been so sure I would be on board with it, you would have told me from the start, and you didn't. You kept it your dirty little secret."

He flipped the omelet deftly before sipping at his coffee. "The planet is dying, Astoria. This is the only way to save it."

"No, it isn't. This is you playing God," she said.

"Someone has to," he snapped. "Because if there is an actual God, he's long given up on us. He doesn't care if we live or die, Astoria."

He slid the omelet onto a cutting board and cut it in half before placing each half on a plate. He set one plate in front of Tori and the other in front of his chair before sitting beside her. "Eat."

She poked at the omelet with her fork as Francis ate a few bites. She could hear the wind blowing, and a pleased look crossed Francis's face when the windows rattled from the force. "The Solum Winds are even stronger than predicted. That's excellent news for us."

"What do you mean?" she asked.

He finished eating his omelet and pointed to hers. "You really should eat."

"I'm not hungry." She shoved her plate away and picked up her coffee cup. The strong dark liquid gave her a much needed energy boost. "Why do you care about the winds?"

He leaned back in his chair, lacing his fingers across his flat abdomen. "Do you know what Solum means?"

"It's Latin for lonely," she said.

"That's right. The Solum Winds or The Lonely Winds are

similar to the Santa Ana winds but unique in that unlike the Santa Ana winds, which can happen ten to twenty times annually, the Solum Winds only occur once every dozen years. These winds buffet our entire state."

"I don't need a fucking geography lesson," Tori said. "I'm aware of how the Solum Winds work."

Francis laughed. "If you're so smart, then you should know why the Solum Winds are important to me."

She studied him, horrified awareness dawning on her. "You're using the Solum Winds to push the serum over the state."

"Bingo!" He clapped his hands like a proud teacher. "Without the winds, we could only blanket the city. But the Solum Winds will push the serum not just further but faster as well. By next week, the serum will be breathed in by every single person in this state and, potentially, further. Of course, this is still only a hypothesis, but I have an excellent feeling that what we do today will prove my theory correct."

Excitement thick in his voice, he said, "It will be a long and difficult process to push the serum across the world, but I know it will happen. You forcing me to kill Edgar was a costly mistake, but -"

"I didn't force you to kill Edgar," she said. "He saved my life when you tried to kill me. Although I shouldn't be fucking surprised that you change the past to suit your narrative."

"The past is the past," he said with an infuriating shrug. "But killing Edgar was as big of a blow as you stealing my device. I've searched for years for another warlock powerful enough to create more devices and have come up empty."

"Good," Tori said.

His cheeks reddened with anger. "I'm not giving up. I will find another witch or warlock to create more machines, Astoria. Even if I have to travel to the ends of the world to find them."

"You're so fucking crazy," she said.

He sighed and stood up, putting his coffee cup in the sink. "I need you with me on this. Without you by my side, this is a hollow victory."

"I don't care," she said. "You told me that after you release the serum, I can return to living my life with my mate. Is that a lie too?"

"Of course not," he said, but he wouldn't look her in the eye. "It's time to leave. The Solum Winds will only last another day or so, and this morning is the perfect time to release the serum."

"Please don't do this, Francis," she said. "If you ever loved me even a little, you won't do this."

He smiled tenderly at her. "Astoria, I'm doing this because I love you."

CHAPTER 24

"**S**it down before you wear a hole in the floor, Judd." Porter took his arm when Judd walked by him and tugged him toward a bar stool.

"How long does it take to pick up a witch?" Judd grumbled as Hudson placed a cup of coffee on the bar before him.

Porter glanced at his watch. "Elora lives across the city. It'll take them more than twenty minutes."

"It's been nearly an hour," Judd said.

Mal sat on the stool beside him. "They'll be back soon."

"I should have gone with them," Judd fretted. "What if that fucking bird said something to piss her off?"

"I know he's not your favourite, but Ronin can be charming when he wants to be." Bishop joined them and sat next to Mal.

Judd sipped the hot coffee, staring blankly at the television screen over the bar. Porter had muted it, and Judd watched as one of the city's most famous early morning news duo bantered with a woman holding a koala bear.

The front door opened, and relief washed over Judd when Kat walked into the bar, followed by Ronin and Elora.

Lilianna sat on Elora's shoulder, and Bishop chuffed in surprise.

"That's a big fucking crow," Hudson said.

"Be nice to Elora," Judd advised. "That damn crow nearly plucked out my eyeball when I lost my temper with her."

Judd slid off the bar stool and met Elora in the middle of the bar. "Thanks for coming. Sorry it's so early."

She smiled at him. "It's fine. I'm sorry they took Tori."

"So, you know what's going on?" Judd asked.

"We filled her in on the details." Kat took the cup of coffee from Bishop with a grateful nod.

"I acted out the more exciting scenes with hand puppets," Ronin said.

Elora laughed as Judd glared at Ronin before turning to Elora. "Sorry about sending the bird."

"What? Elora loves me. We're new besties. Isn't that right?" Ronin draped his arm over Elora's shoulder in a friendly manner.

"Definitely besties," Elora said with a grin.

Judd waited with delightful anticipation for Lilianna to shred Ronin's face. To his surprise, the crow stared at Ronin but didn't attack.

"Why isn't Lilianna trying to murder him?" Judd said to Elora.

"Because us birds stick together," Ronin said. "She recognizes my awesomeness. Isn't that right, little lady?"

He reached to pet Lilianna, and Judd's bear chuffed happily when Lilianna snapped viciously at Ronin's fingers.

Ronin yanked his hand back and laughed. "We're not at the petting stage of our friendship yet. That's cool."

The bar door opened again, and Briggs ducked into the bar. Hudson strode across the bar to shake his hand.

"Why is Briggs here?" Judd asked.

"I asked him to come in," Mal said.

"Hell of a first assignment," Ronin said. "You assigned me factory security for my first job. Not exactly as exciting as stopping some dude from sterilizing the city."

"You shouldn't have pissed off Kat when you first started then," Bishop said with a grin.

Ronin laughed before slipping his arm around Kat's waist and kissing her. "I won her over eventually."

"What kind of shifters are they?" Elora asked.

"Polar bear," Kat said.

"I should have brought Cece with me. She's obsessed with polar bears," Elora said. "She's been saving for ages for a trip to Alaska. There's some polar bear tour you can do that gets you, like, within twenty-five feet of them."

She glanced at Kat. "Hey, do you think, after all this is over, that maybe one of those guys would be willing to shift for Cece?"

"Not a chance," Porter said as he joined them. "Polar bear shifters aren't known for their generosity toward humans."

"Bummer," Elora said. "Cece would have been so stoked."

She held out her hand toward Porter. "I'm Elora."

"Porter. This is Mal and Bishop, and the two polar bear shifters are Hudson and Briggs." Porter shook her hand as Lilianna cawed a warning.

"Stop it, Lilikins," Elora said.

"How certain are you that the spell you found will break the protection spell around the device?" Mal asked as Hudson and Briggs joined them.

"Fairly certain, but I won't know for sure until I have the device and start the spell," Elora said.

"What do we do if she can't break the spell?" Porter asked.

"We'll cross that bridge when we come to it. Right now, our biggest issue is finding Tori and Francis before he releases the serum across the city," Mal said.

"I should have brought a gas mask." Ronin glanced at Kat. "Your mom will be so mad if little Ronin can't knock you up. I promised her grandkittens."

Mal turned to Judd. "You said that Francis talked about how it was almost too late, right?"

Judd nodded. "Yes, he said time was limited, and they were almost out of time, but now that he had the device, this would all be over by today."

"Okay, we can assume he's setting off the device today," Mal said.

"The grizzly shifter said he was releasing the serum this morning," Judd said.

"He could have already set it off," Hudson said. "We have no fucking way of knowing."

"We do." Judd took out a phone from his jacket pocket. "I took the grizzly shifter's phone. He said Francis would call him when it was done. He hasn't called yet."

"Smart move," Mal said. He stared thoughtfully at Bishop. "We need to figure out why Francis was running out of time. What's happening in the city right now? Any events that would draw large crowds and make it easier for Francis to infect more people at once?"

"The humans for shifters rights rally," Porter said. "Maggie and I had dinner with Mom and Dad the night before last, and Mom was talking about the rally. She's a guest speaker at it."

"Where is it happening?" Mal asked.

"Downtown at nine this morning. Mom said they're expecting a good turnout of humans. If this Francis guy wants to infect a bunch of humans and shifters rapidly, this could be the way."

"You said this machine was pretty small, right?" Elora said.

Judd turned to her. "Yeah. No bigger than about eighteen by eighteen inches."

"But Francis is planning on sterilizing the entire city with it?"

"Yes," Judd said. "Tori told me that the serum will stay in the atmosphere for at least forty-eight hours."

"It's a big city and a small machine," Elora said. "They'd need to set off the machine in multiple places to cover the entire place, right?"

"Maybe, maybe not," Mal said. "When magic is involved, anything is possible."

"That's sort of true," Elora said. "This warlock most likely used magic to boost the machine's abilities. But even magic has its boundaries and limitations, and if you push it too far beyond what it's meant to do, things get real weird, real fast. Any witch or warlock worth their salt knows you can't force magic to go further than it should or what your abilities can control."

"So, you're saying this warlock wasn't powerful enough to build a machine that would blanket the entire city in the serum?" Judd said. "Because Francis told Tori that he had."

"I think Francis was lying. The warlock would need to be incredibly powerful to do that," she said, "and, honestly, they're rare. Not just that, but they have a hard time flying under the radar if they're that powerful. The WWC closely monitors witches and warlocks with a certain level of power."

"Like your grandmother?" Kat asked.

Elora studied her. "What do you know about my grandmother?"

Kat shrugged. "I have a cousin who got caught up with the Fae. She eventually went to your grandmother for help."

"Shit, she's Helen's granddaughter?" Bishop stared at Elora with new appreciation. "Are you as powerful as she is?"

"No," Elora said. "My point is, the WWC would have been keeping a close eye on this Edgar dude if he was that powerful. There's no way he could have done that much dark magic without them knowing about it and stopping it. Which means Francis probably needs to set the machine off at multiple locations."

"Question," Briggs said. "What's the WWC?"

"Witches and Warlocks Council. They govern the use of magic," Elora said.

"If Francis is planning on using multiple locations, why was he talking about time running out then?" Mal mused.

Elora studied the television behind the bar. "That was my question too. This Francis guy is evil but smart, right? He knows that if he has to set off the machine at multiple places, the chances of him being caught increase substantially. People will notice some dude spraying purple mist into the air. The warlock probably wasn't powerful enough to create a machine that sterilizes the entire city in one go, but something else is."

"What are you trying to say, little witch?" Briggs asked.

Elora pointed to the screen. "The Solum Winds."

Judd and the others turned to look at the screen. A female reporter stood at the edge of Parsons Cliff. Parsons Cliff was located in Parsons Woods, and the rocky edge jutted out over Hayes River that wound through the forest. In the summer, it was a popular place for hikers to take in the spectacular view of the forest beyond the cliff.

The reporter clung to her microphone, squinting her eyes

as a massive gust of wind whipped her blonde hair around her face, and the sun rose behind her. The wind kicked up little puffs of snow until it looked like she stood in the middle of a mini-blizzard. Porter grabbed the remote and unmuted the television.

"Parsons Cliff is one of the most popular places in the city. Even in the winter, there are usually tourists and hiking enthusiasts roaming the cliff's edge and taking in the majestic view. But this popular tourist destination has been abandoned for the last few days. Marked as the spot where the Solum Winds are strongest, few people want to brave the cold or risk being blown off the cliff." The reporter made a short 'eep' into the microphone when a violent gust of wind made her stagger.

She glanced at the cliff edge behind her before inching closer to the camera. "The Solum Winds are at their strongest today and have already been recorded at twenty-five miles per hour in some areas of the city. Here at Parsons Cliff, it's predicted the Solum Winds could get up to fifty-two miles per hour in the next few hours." The reporter staggered again as another gust of wind made the trees sway behind her and kicked up a mini-tornado of snowflakes.

"The good news is the winds should start dying down later this afternoon and be completely gone by the end of the week." The reporter grimaced when a chunk of ice smacked into her leg and then plastered a smile on her face. "This is Melissa North for CFTC, reporting live from Parsons Cliff."

The view switched to the morning anchors, and the man turned to his co-host. "Goodness, Joan, I can say that I am delighted to be here in the warm studio this morning."

"Agreed, Jim." His co-anchor smiled into the camera, her teeth a brilliant white and her skin an unnatural orange. "The Solum Winds have dropped the temperature by seventeen degrees this morning, so make sure you bundle up for your drive to work."

Porter muted the television as Elora said, "If you wanted to sterilize an entire city using a weird mist, wouldn't you look at using nature to help? The Solum Winds are highest at Parsons Cliff. Releasing the serum from that location would guarantee the winds would spread it across the city. And it explains why Francis is on a time limit and is determined to release the serum this morning. The winds start to die down by this afternoon."

Judd stared at Elora. "Holy fuck, I could kiss you right now."

She grinned at him. "Not gonna lie, I'd be into that, but I'm pretty sure Lilianna would murder you if you did."

Ronin laughed. "Probably best to stay away from her, big guy. You know us birds tend to get the best of you."

Judd's bear growled in annoyance as Mal said, "With Solum Winds that strong, he could cover more than the city with serum. We leave for Parsons Cliff now. If we're lucky, we'll get there before Francis does and can be ready to take him and his people out before he sets off the device."

"So, we're just assuming that Elora is right?" Porter asked. "No offense, but it's a huge assumption to make. What if Francis isn't using the winds to distribute the serum. We're at Parsons Cliff freezing our asses off while he's somewhere else in the city releasing the serum and sterilizing a fuck of a lot of people. We should at least send some of your people to the rally, just in case."

"I think Elora's theory is a solid one, but I see your point, Porter. We'll have people at the rally as well." Mal glanced at Judd. "How many shifters would Francis bring with him to the Cliff?"

"I have no fucking idea," Judd said. "He could bring a

hundred, or he could bring a couple. I have no clue how his mind works."

Mal turned to Bishop. "Maybe we should call Garth and Fenton. Get them to meet us at the base of the Cliff."

"The mad scientist might overlook the scent of bears and wolves in the woods," Ronin said, "even a random human, but if he smells a cheetah shifter or a bull shifter? It's going to make him suspicious."

"He's right," Hudson said.

"That means you're out too, Kitten," Ronin said to Kat.

She hissed at him, and he winked at her. "You know I'm right."

"He is," Mal said. "Sorry, Kat, but you're sitting this one out."

"And if this Francis guy brings a dozen or more shifters? Then what?" Kat asked.

"We've got Big White and his new friend," Ronin said. "Those two could probably take out a dozen shifters alone."

Mal turned to Porter. "You and Kat will stay here with Elora and -"

"Oh, no fucking way, Mal," Porter said. "Tori isn't just an employee. She's a friend too. Not to mention that Judd saved my life. I owe him."

"No, you don't," Judd said.

"I'm not staying here," Porter said.

All right," Mal said. "Kat, you stay here with Elora. We'll call as soon as we have the device."

"I'm going with you," Elora said. "The sooner I break the spell, the better."

"We'll bring the device to you," Mal said.

"Unless you fail," she said bluntly. "I'm just as invested as the rest of you in destroying this machine. I might be young, but I want kids eventually, and I don't want to be involved in a futuristic *Thunderdome* situation with other females to win the right to bang the one dude left in the city with working sperm."

"We should role play *Thunderdome* tonight," Ronin said to Kat. "You can be Mad Max, and I'll be the sexy but dangerous Tina Turner who can't resist luring you into my pleasure dome."

"Jesus," Hudson said. "Keep it in your fucking pants, bird."

"I'm going to the Cliff with you," Elora said. "You can't stop me."

Mal grimaced but said, "Briggs and Hudson, keep Elora between you at all times. Don't let anyone near her while she's breaking the spell."

"I'll call Fenton, Davis, and a few others," Kat said. "We'll hit the rally and look for Francis. Judd, I'll need you to give me a description of what he looks like."

Mal glanced at his watch. "All right, we have a plan. Let's get to work, people."

CHAPTER 25

"**D**on't you think you went a little overboard with the shifters?" Tori's foot slipped, and she nearly landed on her ass.

Francis glanced behind them at the dozen shifters who trudged through the trees. Most were bear shifters, but there were several wolf shifters and a couple of hyena shifters. "Safety first, Astoria."

"Safety against what?" Tori said. "We're out in the middle of the goddamn woods, hiking up a fucking cliff. I know you're a cowardly antelope, but I think one or two shifters would have been enough to protect you from predators roaming the woods."

Francis laughed. "You think insulting me upsets me, but it doesn't. You can pretend you hate me, but deep down inside, you respect what I'm doing and know it's the right thing."

"No, I fucking don't," she spat.

"What I'm about to do will change the course of history," Francis said. "I can't be stingy about my safety at a time like this."

"Nobody knows where the fuck you are or what you're going to do," Tori said.

Francis just gave her an infuriating grin and lapsed into silence. Tori studied the trees around her before glancing at Jaden. The jaguar shifter curled his lip at her. "Run, and your little bear boyfriend is dead."

"Your henchmen need to work on their social skills," Tori told Francis.

He laughed. "Henchmen? God, don't be so dramatic, Astoria. Jaden is my head of security, a position you used to hold. Did you consider yourself my henchman?"

"I considered myself your friend until you lied to me and tried to kill me," Tori said.

"Pobody's nerfect," Francis said cheerfully before laughing.

The wind tore the laughter out of his mouth and carried it away before making its own howling moan that made Tori's bunny thump with unease. They were close to the top of the cliff now, and the wind raged through the trees. A violent gust of wind nearly blew her off her feet, and she yanked away from Jaden's grip when he grabbed her arm.

He snarled at her, his hand tightening on her bicep. "C'mon, little bunny, the boss will be pissed if you blow away."

Francis, his head bent into the wind, adjusted the messenger bag around his body. He'd slipped the device into the bag after they'd parked their vehicles at the forest's edge. They'd been hiking for nearly forty minutes, and despite her winter boots and jacket, Tori felt like a frozen slab of meat.

She hiked after Francis, her eyes watering from the gritty snow being blown into her face. The terrain grew steadily steeper, and the slippery snow and uneven terrain made her quads burn.

By the time they made it to the top of the cliff, all of them were panting, and a couple of the bear shifters looked like they were about to pass out. Tori walked closer to the edge and peered over it, studying the rushing, flowing river below. Her bunny thumped nervously. Over the years, more than one hiker had fallen to their death after stepping too close to the edge, and while Tori didn't like the idea of being smashed to death by the jagged rocks lining the river's edge, she also didn't care much for living the rest of her life forced to do Francis's bidding. Death would be preferable.

What about Judd? Francis will eventually let down his guard, and you can escape. You did it once before. You can do it again. But if you jump off this damn cliff, you'll never see your mate again.

She would never see him again anyway. Francis would kill Judd if he hadn't killed him already. Why not join her mate in the afterlife?

You don't know he's dead! Her bunny was freaking the fuck out, her thumping so loud it made Tori's brain hurt. She rubbed at her temples, muttering an apology to her bunny. A wild gust of wind shoved her in the back like a giant's hand, and she stumbled forward, her eyes widening as she teetered on the cliff's edge.

Oh fuck, she really was about to die.

Another gust of wind pushed her past her balance point, and she cried out when a hard hand grabbed her by the shoulder and yanked her back before she could tumble off the cliff.

"Jesus, you got a fucking death wish, you dumb bunny?" Jaden glared at her and shoved her away from the edge.

His face white, Francis said, "Stay right beside me, Astoria, or I'll have Jaden tie you to a fucking tree."

She joined Francis about ten feet from the edge as the

other shifters made a loose half-circle behind them. Francis slipped the messenger bag over his head and set it on the ground before taking out the device. He used his hand to clear the skiff of snow covering the rocky ground and set the device down gently.

He straightened and sucked in a deep breath before frowning and staring at the trees behind them.

"What is it, boss?" Jaden joined them.

"I smell wolf and bear," Francis said.

Jaden nodded. "The woods are full of them."

Francis studied the other shifters, and Jaden clapped him on the shoulder. "Relax. There's more than enough of us to keep you safe. Besides, push that damn button, and we can be out of here in five minutes."

"Do they know what will happen when you push that button?" Tori pointed to the shifters. She raised her voice over the howling of the wind. "Do they know you're about to fucking sterilize them?"

They stared impassively at her, and Francis laughed. "Of course they do, Astoria. You can't turn them against me."

Francis crouched next to the machine. Her heart racing, Tori said, "Wait!"

"For fuck's sake. I'm freezing my nutsack off here. Shut the fuck up and let him get on with it before we all freeze to death," Jaden said.

"I want proof of life," Tori said.

Francis straightened. The tips of his ears were bright red, and his breath plumed out to mix with hers. "I told you, I'll let your boyfriend go as soon as we finish here."

"Call first. Prove to me that Judd's alive, Francis."

"Or what?" Jaden said. "You don't hold a single card here, sweetheart. So, just shut your mouth and enjoy the show."

He shoved her in the back, pitching her forward into Francis. Francis helped her straighten before glaring at Jaden. "Enough, asshole. Give me my phone."

Jaden rolled his eyes but handed Francis his phone. Francis pressed a button and held the phone to his ear. Her body shaking with the cold, Tori blew on her hands as lines appeared between Francis's eyebrows.

"Do you hear that?" he asked Jaden.

Jaden cocked his head. "Hear what?"

"Ringing," Francis said.

Jaden gave him an odd look before pointing to his phone. "Yeah, from the phone."

"No, it's…." Still holding his phone, Francis turned in a circle, smelling the air with his head cocked.

The wind died off slightly, and Tori's eyes widened when she heard the ringing from the trees. Her bunny hopped around excitedly when Judd emerged from the trees, a phone held in one hand.

"You looking for me?" he asked before dropping the phone in the snow.

"Judd," Tori said.

"What the fuck?" Francis said.

"Kill that motherfucker!" Jaden roared before shoving Tori to the ground and stepping in front of Francis. He shifted to his jaguar with a pop as the roar of a grizzly echoed in the trees.

A giant grizzly bear with dark brown fur appeared beside Judd. He roared again, his fangs gleaming in the sunlight as a gray wolf and a brown wolf stepped out of the woods and flanked the grizzly. They snarled at the shifters still standing in a semi-circle as Judd shifted to his bear.

Jaden howled, and the sound knocked Francis's shifters from their stupor. One by one, they shifted to their animal forms as Judd, the grizzly, and the wolves ran toward them. Tori scrambled to her feet and dove for the device, screaming in pain when a hyena shifter darted forward and clamped down on her left arm, sinking his fangs through the material of her jacket and into her flesh.

She heard Judd's roar of anger as she punched the hyena in the head with her free hand. It yelped but held on grimly, and with another shriek, she gouged at his eye with her thumb. The hyena howled and released her. She fell back, hot blood flowing down her arm. Blood oozing from his eye, the hyena growled and crouched to leap, yelping in pain when the black bear's massive paw slammed down on his back and drove him to the ground. The hyena writhed beneath the bear's grip, his paws scrabbling at the rocky ground as the bear roared again before biting into the back of the hyena's skull. The hyena died instantly, his body going limp, and the bear growled happily.

Tori stared up at the black bear. "Hello, my bear."

Judd chuffed to her, and she reached out with her uninjured hand. Before she could touch his thick fur, a dark gray grizzly shifter plowed into Judd, sending him tumbling across the ground. The two bears fought viciously as a hand gripped her arm and pulled her to her feet.

"Ronin?" She stared at the bird shifter.

"Hey, how's it going?" Ronin grinned at her as the snarls and growls echoed around them. "Some fucking wind, huh?"

"The device. We need to get the device before Francis pushes that fucking button," she said.

"On it," Ronin said. He ran toward the device, snatching it from the ground just as Francis dove for it.

"Jaden!" Francis screamed. "He has the device!"

Jaden turned and bared his fangs at Ronin before stalking toward him, his tail swishing back and forth.

"Good kitty," Ronin said as he pulled a large knife from a sheath on his belt and backed away. "How about I find you a catnip toy, and you play with that instead of my intestines? Although, just between you and me, I smoked enough weed last night that I'd probably get you as stoned as the old nip."

Jaden hissed and leaped at him. Moving fast, Ronin dodged to the right, and Jaden landed with an angry snarl on the cold ground.

"Catch, little bunny!" Ronin shouted before throwing the device at Tori.

Her arm screaming at her, she caught the box, nearly dropping it on the ground when her bloody hand slid across the smooth metal.

"Nice recovery!" Ronin hollered as Jaden jumped on him. Before Ronin could shove the knife into Jaden's ribs, the jaguar ripped out Ronin's throat with ruthless efficiency. Ronin dropped like a stone, blood pouring from his throat and dead before he touched the ground. Jaden yowled in victory and turned to face Tori, his tail snapping back and forth.

"Shit," Tori said as Jaden bared his fangs at her.

"Tori! Over here!" Elora's voice could be barely heard over the wind.

Jaden ran toward her as Tori turned. Elora stood a few feet away, flanked by Hudson and Briggs in their polar bear forms.

"Catch!" Tori shouted and chucked the device at Elora. The witch caught it, and Tori dived to the right just as Jaden pounced. She landed with a thud on her injured left arm but ignored the pain as she jumped up.

Jaden had lost interest in her, his green eyes glowing as he hissed at the two polar bear shifters. They made twin growls, and Jaden hesitated as Elora set the device on the ground, held her hands over it, and began to chant. The wind carried away her voice, and Tori could only fucking hope that Elora had the right spell as Mal and a white wolf fought viciously just to her right.

"Get the device!" Francis screamed. He cowered near the cliff's edge, his antlers poking through his skull and brown fur covering most of his face.

Jaden stared at the two polar bears before backing away.

"No!" Francis shrieked.

Jaden ignored him and turned to leap onto Bishop's back. Bishop roared with pain, his big paw swiping uselessly at the jaguar. Before Jaden could sink his teeth into the back of Bishop's neck, Judd tore him off and threw him to the ground.

The jaguar bounced to his feet, and he and Judd circled each other as two black bears went after Bishop.

Fuck! Tori didn't want to admit it, but they were losing. Bishop and the others were fighting hard, but they were outnumbered.

She turned to the polar bear shifters. They stared as anxiously as she did at the others, and she ran to them. "Go. I'll protect Elora."

They didn't move, and she slapped Hudson impatiently on one big shoulder. "Fucking go, Hudson! They'll die if the two of you don't help!"

With a low roar, Hudson and Briggs ran toward the other shifters. Tori stood in front of Elora. Elora didn't look up as she continued the incantation. Despite the cold, sweat dripped down her forehead, and her small body swayed with the force of the wind as blue light glowed from her hands.

The low growl behind Tori sent her adrenaline into overdrive. She turned, staring at the jaguar as he stalked toward her. Her heart dropped to the damn snow at her feet... had Jaden killed Judd? Jaden's side bled profusely from deep claw marks, and he limped badly on his right back leg. She bent and pried a rock from the cold ground, holding it in her good hand. She winced when Ronin's dead body caught fire and hoped like hell that the stories about phoenix shifters rising from the ash weren't just a myth.

Jaden glanced at the flames before dismissing them and turning back to face her. He hissed and bared his fangs, his tail flicking rapidly.

"What the fuck are you waiting for, asshole?" Tori shouted. "You want the device? Come fucking get it!"

Jaden crouched, but the giant black crow dive bombed him before he could leap. Cawing loudly, Lilianna attacked Jaden's head, pecking viciously at the jaguar as he roared in pain and swiped one paw at her.

Lilianna flew upward, avoiding his long claws easily as behind Jaden, the red and gold phoenix emerged from the ashes.

Lilianna dive bombed the jaguar again, pecking with deadly accuracy at his face. Jaden howled, and Lilianna cawed in triumph before soaring into the air with Jaden's right eye clamped in her beak.

Blood gushing from his empty eye socket, Jaden yowled and stumbled toward Tori, shaking his head and sending blood droplets flying. Tori raised her rock, but a naked Ronin ran up to the jaguar and yanked his head back by one white fur tipped ear.

"Hey, pretty kitty. I was only playing dead," Ronin said with a grin as he used the blade in his right hand to slice across the jaguar's throat. Blood turned the snow a muddy red, and Jaden collapsed with a muffled thump to the ground.

Lilianna landed on the dead jaguar's back with his eye still clamped in her beak. She cawed before tilting her head back and swallowing the eye.

"Oh God." Ronin retched and bent over with his hands on his knees. "I'm gonna throw up."

Lilianna's cawing almost sounded like laughter as she descended into the air again. She circled above Elora, wings flapping against the wind as Ronin joined Tori. "How the fuck is that bird even flying in this wind?"

Tori searched frantically for Judd, relief pouring through her when she saw him and Porter working together to take down a brown bear shifter. Mal was tearing out the throat of the white wolf, and Hudson and Briggs were fighting grizzly shifters.

"Hot damn, those polar bears can fight," Ronin shouted.

Blue light, so bright and hot it immediately banished the cold from Tori's body, exploded behind them. Elora cried out, and Tori turned, her eyes widening when Elora staggered back and fell to the ground. Her skin matched the snow in colour, and she shook violently as Tori knelt beside her. Lilianna flew down and landed beside Elora, grooming her hair repeatedly as Tori took Elora's hand.

"Elora, are you okay?"

"I'm good," she gasped. "Just tired. I broke the spell."

"Holy fuck," Tori said. "You broke the fucking spell!"

"I broke the fucking spell," Elora said before falling on her back with a groan. "Destroy it. Quickly!"

Lilianna nuzzled Elora's face with her beak as Tori grabbed the device and stood. "Ronin, the spell is broken!"

"Great!" Ronin shouted. "Destroy the fucking thing and - shit! Incoming!"

Ronin shoved her to the side and caught the hyena as it leaped at them. The force knocked him flying, and he shoved one hand under the hyena's jaw, pushing it upward as the hyena snapped at his face.

"Go!" he shouted again before stabbing the hyena with his knife.

Tori took off for the cliff's edge, raising the device over her head. Before she could throw it over the edge, she was spun around by a hard hand on her arm. She had a brief glimpse of Francis's wide-eyed stare before he bent and searing pain speared her stomach.

She stared in numb shock at the top of Francis's head and the two wickedly sharp antlers embedded in her belly. With a soft snort, Francis pulled away, and hot blood spurted out of Tori's stomach and soaked her legs.

Half in his human form and half in his antelope form, Francis reached for the device. Her legs weak, and her ears ringing, Tori punched him in the stomach.

Francis doubled over, coughing and gasping. He stared up at her with watery eyes, his hand reaching for her. "Astoria, don't. Please, you can't -"

He screamed when she tossed the device over the side of the cliff. He staggered to his feet, his eyes wild and more fur sprouting across his face. "What have you done? What have you -"

A wild and heavy gust of wind knocked him back to his knees. It lifted Tori completely off her feet, and she tumbled off the side of the cliff, her reaching, scrambling hand snagging a rock that jutted out from the side. She slammed up against the side of the cliff, the hot pain in her belly making her shriek. She held on grimly, scrabbling with her injured arm to find another rock to grip as her arm muscles screamed in protest. Her feet drummed helplessly against the cliffside, and her hand started to cramp as Francis peered over the side, his antlers still sticking out of his head.

He grinned maniacally, one hand clutching his stomach. "You stupid fucking bitch! You're going to die, and it was for nothing. I'll find another warlock to rebuild the device, and there isn't anything you -"

His eyes widened, and he screamed with terror when Judd, in his bear form, lifted him over his head. With an angry roar, he threw Francis over the cliff. Shrieking wildly, Francis twisted and turned before he landed with a thud on the jagged rocks sticking out from the river's edge.

A hard hand gripped Tori's arm, and she looked away from Francis's mangled body and into Judd's warm brown eyes.

"I have you, my mate," Judd said. "Let go."

She let go, dangling in Judd's grip for a moment before he pulled her easily up the cliff and into his arms. He kissed her, laid her on the ground, and eased up her shirt. Panic blossomed on his face, and he pressed a hand against the wounds in her stomach, making her cry out with pain. "I'm sorry, baby. Hold on. Just hold on. Ronin! Get your ass over here!"

Judd's face and voice faded, and she groped weakly for his hand. "Judd? Honey, don't leave me."

"I'm not, baby. Just stay awake, okay? Ronin! Move your fucking ass!"

Tori squinted at Ronin when he replaced Judd. He dropped to his knees beside her. "Hey, bunny girl. Let's get you fixed up, yeah?"

"Judd," she whispered. "I want Judd."

"I'm right here, baby." Judd's big hand took hers, and he gripped it tightly before kissing her forehead. "I'm not going anywhere, I promise."

Her gaze flickered to Ronin when he leaned over her stomach. Tears caught in his eyelashes before he blinked, and they dropped onto her stomach. Sizzling pain sliced through her, and she screamed hoarsely, her body arching upward as Ronin pinned her down with one hard hand across her stomach.

She screamed again, and when the blackness appeared at the edges of her vision, she dove into its blissful, pain-free depths.

CHAPTER 26

"Don't worry, Lindie-Lou. She'll wake up soon." Judd sat on the side of his bed and petted Linda, who was curled up next to a sleeping Tori. "She's had a hard day and needs her rest, right? It's okay that she didn't wake up after Ronin healed her."

Linda licked his hand, and he petted her again. "If she hasn't woken up in a couple of hours, I'll call that damn bird shifter and tell him to come over and cry on her again."

"Please don't," Tori said in a raspy voice. "You hate him, and you'll never forgive me if you have to let him into your house."

"Tori," Judd breathed before sitting her up and hugging her hard. He winced and let her go. "Shit, I'm sorry. Are you okay? Did that hurt your stomach?"

"I'm fine," she said. "Nothing hurts. I am thirsty, though."

He reached for the water bottle on the nightstand and took off the cap before handing it to her. She drank nearly half of it before wiping her mouth and leaning back against the headboard. "I like your room."

"I almost didn't bring you back to my place," Judd said.

"I figured the dead men we'd left in my kitchen would be pretty ripe by now. But they were gone. The entire kitchen smelled like bleach and not a dead body or drop of blood anywhere."

"Francis always cleans up his mess." She swallowed hard. "I can't believe he's dead."

Judd squeezed her thigh. "I won't apologize for killing him. He would have let you fall to your death, Tori."

"I know," she said. "You did what you had to, and I don't blame you or wish you'd made a different choice. The Francis on that cliff wasn't the Francis that I loved. He died a long time ago."

They sat silently for a few minutes before she took his hand. "Are you okay, my bear?"

"Yes," he said. "Ronin cried on anyone who needed it back at the Cliff."

That made her laugh and Linda nudged at her hand before curling up in her lap. She stroked the dog's soft fur. "I'm happy to see you too, Linda."

"Hudson grabbed our stuff from the motel and brought Linda over about two hours ago," Judd said.

"How did you escape the bear shifters at the farm?" she asked.

"Turns out that mama squirrel shifter is a fucking badass," Judd said. "She killed the black bear shifter, and I killed the grizzly. They were going to kill all of us as soon as Francis called to say he'd released the serum. I took the grizzly's phone when I left so I'd know if fucking Francis had actually released it."

"Seriously?"

Judd nodded. "Yeah, her name is Alice. She said if we survived, to give her a call so we can have dinner at the farm next weekend."

Tori laughed. "I did not expect you to make friends with a squirrel shifter, but it's super cute that you did. How did you know we'd be at Parsons Cliff?"

"Elora," Judd said. "She thought Francis was lying about how powerful the warlock was and that he would need the Solum Winds to blanket the entire city with the serum. It was the best theory we had, so we went with it."

"He wasn't lying about Edgar's power," Tori said. "He wanted to use the Solum Winds to blanket the entire state."

"Jesus," Judd said.

"How long have I been out?" she asked.

"Nearly six hours," he said. "When you didn't wake up after Ronin healed you, he said to take you home and let you sleep. He said you were fully healed, but…."

"I am," she assured him.

"You nearly died," he said. "Francis gored you deep with his antlers, and then you almost fell off the side of the fucking cliff. If I hadn't gotten there in time…."

"You did, my bear." She leaned forward and cupped his face, stroking his beard with her fingers. "I'm fine."

He sucked in a deep breath. He couldn't articulate how it felt to watch Tori tumble off that cliff. How breathtakingly deep his terror had been when he thought she was dead.

"I love you," he said.

Her smile widened. "I love you too. Now, tell me what happened after you saved me."

"Hudson and Bishop killed the last two shifters while Ronin healed you," Judd said. "Then he healed anyone else who needed it, and we got the fuck off that cliff."

"Is Elora okay?" Tori asked.

"She's fine. Exhausted and nearly frozen to the bone, but we sat her between Hudson and Briggs on the ride back to the bar, and she warmed up pretty quick. Kat and Ronin took her back to her place, and Kat said they would stay with her for a few hours to make sure she was okay."

A small grin crossed his face. "She said to tell you she'd square up payment with you later this week."

Tori laughed. "Why do I feel like she'll charge me double?"

"She probably will. Anyway, everyone else is fine. Porter said we don't have to return to work until we're ready."

"That was nice of him," Tori said.

"Yeah," Judd said. "He and Mal and Bishop left to talk to that detective friend of theirs. Bren something or other."

She tensed, and he took her hand, squeezing it lightly. "Mal said Bren would want to talk to us but that he could guarantee that none of us would be in trouble for what we did."

"If this detective even believes him. What if he just takes a look at all the dead bodies on the cliff and decides to arrest all of us?"

"He won't," Judd said. "I know it's hard for you to trust people, but Mal says Bren is on our side, and I believe him."

Tori stared at their linked hands. "So, now what?"

"Now you get to have a life again," Judd said. "No more running, no more hiding, no more pretending to be someone you aren't."

She traced his knuckles with her thumb. "What about us?"

Judd could hear the trepidation in her voice. He shooed Linda off her lap, pulled back the quilt, and lifted Tori into his lap. He cupped her face and pressed a kiss against her mouth. "You're my mate, Tori, and I love you. I want to spend the rest of my life with you."

She blinked rapidly, tears shining in her eyes. "I love you too, Judd. So much."

He kissed her again, their tongues touching delicately. She sighed into his mouth and ran her hands over his broad shoulders. "You're a great kisser."

He laughed. "So, are you. You're moving in with me."

She blinked at him. "That seems quick."

"No, what will seem quick is when I go out tomorrow and buy you an engagement ring," he said.

Her mouth dropped open. "You're fucking joking."

"Nope," he said. "We don't have to get married immediately, but I want everyone to know you're mine."

"Yours," she said softly. "I like being yours."

"I like it too," he said.

She relaxed in his arms, tracing her fingers over his broad chest. "I can't believe it's finally over."

"It's over," he said, placing a finger under her chin and tipping her head up. "Now it's just you and me spending the rest of our lives together in peace and quiet."

She grinned at him. "You don't actually believe the peace and quiet part, do you?"

He laughed and kissed her again. "Nope, but it sounded good, right?"

"It sounded perfect," she said before sliding her arms around his shoulders. "Now, strip off those clothes and show me how much you love me."

"Whatever you say, Tori-girl."

"HELLO, MY BEAR." TORI CLIMBED INTO THE VEHICLE BEFORE leaning over and kissing Judd. "Thank you for picking me up."

"Hi. How'd it go?" Judd asked.

"Good," Tori said.

Judd waited for a beat. "I'll need a little more than good. Did they offer you a job?"

Tori grinned at him. "They did. I start on Monday. Although they're having a staff meeting on Friday, and Mal asked me to come in so I could meet everyone else."

Judd whooped loudly and pounded the steering wheel with his fist before leaning over and kissing her hard. "I knew you'd get the job! Congratulations!"

"Thank you. Working for Burke, King, and Frost Securities feels a little more in my wheelhouse than being a server at a bar does."

Judd squeezed her hand before he started the car and pulled out onto the street. "I'm proud of you, baby."

"Thanks. I'm just glad Porter wasn't upset about me quitting the bar."

Judd shook his head. "Once he found out you were an assassin, there was no way he believed you'd keep working at the bar."

She rolled her eyes. "If you keep calling me an assassin, I'll make you go without sex for a week."

"No, you won't," he said smugly. "You can't resist all this." He pointed to his body and winked suggestively at her.

She reached across and tugged on one of his barbells through his t-shirt. His nostrils flared, and he gave her a look. "Keep doing that, and I'll ditch our plans and take you straight home to bed."

"Maybe we should," she said. "We can do this another day."

He squeezed her hand again as he drove through the city. "I know you're nervous and worried that she'll be upset, but I don't think she will be. I think she'll just be happy."

"What if she isn't?" Tori said. "What if she hates me and never wants to speak to me again?"

"That won't happen." He kissed her knuckles before taking a right.

Her bunny thumped excitedly at the familiar street, but nausea swirled in Tori's belly. "Judd, I don't know if I can do this."

"You can," he said. "I know you can, baby."

She took a deep breath, drawing strength from his touch and quiet confidence. By the time they parked in front of the house, she was mostly breathing normally and almost seventy-five percent sure she wouldn't vomit.

Judd stepped out of the car, and she opened her door and stepped out into the cold air. She studied the house, her nerves jangling in her belly, as Judd took her hand.

"You can do this," he said. "She'll be happy, baby."

Holding Judd's hand tightly, she followed him to the house. They climbed the porch stairs, and she jerked when Judd knocked on the door. He squeezed her hand again. "Take a deep breath, Tori-girl."

She sucked in a lungful of cold air, releasing it in a harsh rush when the door opened, and the small, delicate-looking woman stared up at Judd. "Can I help you?"

"Hi, Mom," Tori said.

Her mother's gaze flickered to her, and surprise washed over her face. "Astoria?"

"Hi," Tori said.

There was a moment of awkward silence before her mother burst into tears and threw herself at Tori. Tori caught her and hugged her hard, burying her face in her mom's neck. She could smell her mother's happiness as her mom leaned back and cupped her face. She studied her for a few seconds before smiling. "I've missed you, sweet girl."

"I've missed you too. I'm so sorry I stayed away, but I swear there was a good reason for it."

Her mom squeezed her face. "I'm just happy to see you again. But come inside, and you can tell me everything."

"Okay. Mom, I want you to meet someone. This is my mate, Judd."

Her mom smiled up at him, her nose twitching rapidly. "A bear shifter?"

Judd nodded. "It's nice to meet you, ma'am."

Her smile widened. "I always knew my girl would fall for a predator. Come inside, both of you, before you freeze to death."

She stepped into the house, hurrying down the hall toward the kitchen, as Tori paused in the doorway. She stared up at Judd, her love for him making her feel weak and silly in all the right ways. "I love you so much, Judd."

His gaze softened, and his big hand smoothed back a stray strand of her hair. "I love you too, Tori-girl."

Keep reading for an excerpt of the Shifters Series, Book Ten, "Elora and the Crow" coming soon!

ELORA AND THE CROW EXCERPT

SHIFTERS SERIES, BOOK TEN

Elora set the mortar on the altar and lit the three black candles, studying the spell book in the dim light. "Okay, Lilianna, come here."

The crow flew from her perch atop the bookshelf and settled beside the burning candles on the altar. Elora slipped into her robe and buttoned it before pulling her hair into a loose bun at the top of her head.

"I think this is the one," she said to Lilianna before reaching out and smoothing the crow's midnight black feathers with her fingertips. Lilianna rubbed her beak along her fingers, and Elora smiled before dipping her fingers into the stone mortar and scooping up some of the flower paste. Lilianna cawed indignantly and backed away with wings flapping when Elora tried to smear the paste on her head.

"Look, I get that you hate being dirty, but if you don't let me do this, the spell won't work," Elora said.

With a very human look of resignation, Lilianna took several steps forward, her talons clicking on the wooden altar.

Elora smeared the flower paste along Lilianna's head and down her back as Lilianna made another soft caw of disgust.

"Hang in there, Miss Prissy," Elora said with a laugh, but the laugh sounded nervous and shrill even to her. Lilianna cocked her head, staring quietly at her with her dark eyes.

Elora sighed. "Yeah, okay, I'm nervous. This is a super old spell, and I'm not entirely certain it's the right one. I don't want to turn you into something else by accident."

Lilianna made the rattling/clicking sound she did only when she and Elora were alone. While she didn't specifically know if this was true or not, Elora had always thought that the clicking was Lilianna's way of trying to soothe Elora when she was upset.

She wiped the paste from her fingers and stroked Lilianna's sleek chest. "This will work, sweetie. I know it will. Are you ready?"

Lilianna cawed and nibbled at Elora's fingers. Taking another deep breath, Elora turned to the spell book and spoke the incantation. As she recited the words, she could feel the intoxicating power building inside her. Her pale cheeks flushed with colour, and she stared with wonderment at the blue light glowing from her hands. The power grew stronger, an addictive rush that Elora could chase forever and never tire of. Nothing felt as good to her as performing magic.

She chanted the spell a second time and then a third time until the candle flames burned so brightly she had to squint. The blue light surrounding her hands pulsed and deepened, and an answering glow of blue emanated from the paste on Lilianna's head and back.

Lilianna stared into the candlelight, her dark eyes reflecting the flames. Sweat dripping down her back and her whole body trembling, Elora shouted, "By my power, flame and flower, return her to her genuine form."

Blue light shot out from Elora's hands and bathed Lilianna in its soft glow. Lilianna cawed, the sound filled with pain.

Elora winced but shouted again, "By my power, flame and flower, return her to her genuine form!"

The power surged within her. Her heart rate shot up, and her hands shook wildly as her entire body flooded with the electrifying and oh-so-addictive magic that ran through her blood.

"By my power, flame and flower, return her to her genuine form!" Elora shrieked as Lilianna screamed, and the blue light surrounding her turned blinding.

Lights exploded in Elora's head, and pain instantly annihilated the power. She screamed and grabbed at her skull, falling to her knees as the agony made her back bow and her teeth snap together with a hard click that she felt more than heard.

The pain swelled in her head until she was sure she would die. That her brain would simply turn to jelly and ooze out her ears. She cried out when the brain-melting pain disappeared as quickly as it appeared, and she collapsed on the floor before the altar.

She kept her eyes closed. The only sound was her harsh panting and the faint rock music drifting through the ceiling from her neighbours upstairs.

"Shit, that hurt," she groaned, rubbing tentatively at her temple. "I think I might have given myself brain damage. At the very least I …"

She sat up straight, staring frantically at the altar. "Lilikins! Lilipad, are you… well, shit."

Still very much in her crow form, Lilianna sat on the altar, staring unblinkingly at her.

"It didn't work," Elora said. "I can't believe it didn't work."

Lilianna cawed softly as Elora crawled over to her. She was at eye level with Lilianna, and she gave the crow a glum look. "I'm so sorry, honey. I really thought this would do it."

Lilianna stretched forward and groomed Elora's hair with her beak before spreading her wings and shaking her body. Wet and sticky flower paste splatted Elora's face, and she wrinkled her nose. "I deserved that."

Dejected beyond belief, she blew out the candles and climbed to her feet. Dizziness washed over her, and she grabbed the altar, steadying herself as she took a few deep breaths. Lilianna landed on her shoulder, clicking softly at her, and Elora nodded. "Yeah, I'm okay. Just kind of exhausted. I've never felt the magic so strongly before. I can't believe the spell didn't work."

She stared at the altar and then the ceiling. "At least I didn't singe the ceiling or set anything on fire this time, right?"

Lilianna groomed her hair again, and Elora patted her sleek feathers. "C'mon, Lilipad. It's late. Let's have a shower and go to bed."

Elora was much too hot. She shoved the quilt to her waist, but even the cool bedroom air didn't help. Lilianna was crowded against her back, and the bird was even warmer than usual.

"Lilikins, move back," she muttered, burrowing her head deeper into the pillow.

Lilianna snored softly before flinging one arm over Elora's waist and cupping her breast. She elbowed the bird in the stomach. "Lilianna, you're too hot. Are you trying to set me on…"

Elora's eyes popped open, and she stared at the big hand cupping her breast through her sleep shirt. The fingers were long with short blunt nails, and thick blue veins ran across the back of the hand.

Her sleepiness evaporated, and she turned her head, the tendons in her neck creaking like an old barn door and stared at the man pressed up behind her in the bed.

"What the fuck?" she whispered.

She studied his face in confusion, her gaze traveling over his sharp cheekbones, wide nose, and square jaw. Dark stubble covered his skin, and his narrow lips were relaxed in sleep. His ink-coloured hair was thick and on the longish side, curling at the nape of his neck and around his ears.

"I'm having a dream," Elora said, her voice faint and full of shock. "Time to wake up, Elora."

The man's eyes blinked open. He stared at her, his irises so dark, it was almost impossible to tell where they ended, and his pupils began. He smiled sleepily at her, revealing straight white teeth, before leaning forward and rubbing his nose along her hair.

He froze, his eyes widening and his hand tightening on her breast. He stared at Elora before releasing her and lifting his hand into the air. He stared at it like he'd never seen a human hand before as Elora slid out of bed on legs that felt like rubber bands.

She stumbled away as the man jumped out of bed and whooped loudly. "Holy fuck, you did it!"

She shrieked when he ran across the room and picked her up, hugging her tight and whirling her around until she pounded on his back. He set her down and cupped her face, his eyes wide with delight. "You did it! You fucking did it, you beautiful, wonderful, amazing little witch!"

He gave her a hard, smacking kiss before letting her go and dancing around her bedroom. She backed away and reached for her ninth-grade spelling bee trophy on the bookshelf near the bathroom door. She raised it over her head. "Get out of my apartment, you naked dancing weirdo."

The man stopped dancing. "Elora, it's me."

Elora didn't want to stare at his naked body. She especially didn't want to stare at his dick. But it was kind of hard not to when he had the abs of a bodybuilder and the dick of a porn star.

The man either didn't notice or didn't care that she was staring at his dick. He put his hands up in an 'I'm perfectly sane and not at all dangerous' gesture and said, "Elora, it's me. Lilianna."

Shock washed over her in a tidal wave, and she sagged against the wall, her trembling legs no longer able to support her weight. "Lilianna?"

He nodded. "Yes. The spell worked, little Elora. You've turned me back."

"I, but you… you're a boy," she said.

He grinned. "You noticed."

Her gaze dipped to his cock again, and when it visibly hardened, her cheeks went hot and scarlet. "You're supposed to be a witch. A female witch."

"Surprise," he said.

She stared into those midnight dark eyes, feeling like she teetered at the edge of a deep chasm. She opened her mouth and then closed it. She opened it again, and he gave her an encouraging look. "Are you okay, little witch?"

She swallowed hard and said, "I showered with you."

ABOUT THE AUTHOR

Elizabeth Kelly was born and raised in Ontario, Canada. She moved west as a teenager and now lives in Alberta with her husband and a menagerie of pets. She firmly believes that a person can survive solely on sushi and coffee, and only her husband's mad cooking skills prevents her from proving that theory.

For more information about Elizabeth, check out her website at

www.elizabethkelly.ca

facebook.com/EKellyBooks
twitter.com/ElizabethKBooks
instagram.com/elizabethkelly_author
amazon.com/Elizabeth-Kelly/e/B00EOHZ0MS
bookbub.com/authors/elizabeth-kelly

ALSO BY ELIZABETH KELLY

Tempted Series

Tempted

Twice Tempted

Forever Tempted

Breathless

Tempted Trilogy (Books 1-3)

Red Moon Series

Red Moon

Red Moon Rising

Dark Moon

Alpha Moon

Pale Moon

The Recruit Series

The Recruit (Book One)

The Recruit (Book Two)

The Recruit (Book Three)

The Recruit (Book Four)

The Recruit (Book Five)

The Recruit (Book Six)

The Shifters Series

Willow and the Wolf (Book One)

Ava and the Bear (Book Two)

Katarina and the Bird (Book Three)

Porter's Mate (Book Four)

Bria and the Tiger (Book Five)

Rosalie Undone (Book Six)

The Dragon's Mate (Book Seven)

Rise of the Jaguar (Book Eight)

The Assassin and the Bear (Book Nine)

The Draax Series

Reign (Book One)

Rule (Book Two)

Rebel (Book Three)

Surrender (Book Four)

Harmony Falls Series

Sweet Harmony (Book One)

Perfect Harmony (Book Two)

Forbidden Harmony (Book Three)

Redeeming Harmony (Book Four)

Absolute Harmony (Novella)

Seasoned Romance Series

Bet Your Heart on Me (Book One)

Take a Chance on Me (Book Two)

Individual Books

The Necessary Engagement

Amelia's Touch

The Rancher's Daughter

Healing Gabriel

The Contract

A Home for Lily

Saving Charlotte

Shameless

The Fairy Tales Collection

Broken

An Unlikely Seduction

Holiday Romance

The Christmas Wife

The Christmas Rescue

The Christmas Nanny

The Christmas Boss

Sordid Games